THE VAULT

Before them stood a powerfully-fortified door, behind which lay the document that could bring down the Empire.

"It'll take us a week to figure out how it opens," said the Major.

"Then burn the damned thing down," replied Jules.

The unbelievable fury of heavy-duty beams chewed away at the thick steel plating until the door fell in with a crash. Then, suddenly, a powerful force yanked them all off their feet.

"Ultragrav!" gasped Jules.

They were trapped. All they could do was lie there, pinned to the floor by an artificial force of 25 gravities, and watch the castle guards approach with blasters drawn...

IMPERIAL STARS

E.E. "DOC" SMITH
with STEPHEN GOLDIN

PYRAMID BOOKS NEW YORK

IMPERIAL STARS
A PYRAMID BOOK

Copyright © 1976 by Verna Smith Trestrail

Pyramid edition published February 1976

ISBN 0-515-03839-3

Library of Congress Catalog Card Number: 75-42968

Printed in the United States of America

_____

Pyramid Books are published by Pyramid Communications, Inc. Its trademarks, consisting of the word "Pyramid" and the portrayal of a pyramid, are registered in the United States Patent Office.

Pyramid Communications, Inc., 919 Third Avenue, New York, N.Y. 10022

IMPERIAL
STARS

CHAPTER 1

Three Man

By the year 2447, the Empire of Earth would have looked remarkably healthy to an outside observer. In the almost two centuries since its formation, it had nearly doubled its size in terms of subject planets, while trade between inhabited worlds was proceeding at a smooth and industrious pace. Hunger and need had been, if not obliterated, at least confined to small pockets of despair. Yet even the most vigorous body politic can harbor a cancer that, if not excised quickly, will eat away at the insides and leave just a useless shell as evidence of its passing. Such a cancer was, in that year, threatening the very existence of the Empire. (M'benge, The Empire—Yesterday and Today, slot 437.)

The first man was dressed in black from head to toe, the only break in that color scheme being the goggles over his eyes—and even they were smoky gray. The dark cloth was smooth and pliable; it made not even the slightest swishing sound as he moved.

The man's belt was divided into a series of compartments, each housing a useful and, in several cases, lethal tool. Outside, the clothing was completely insulated against electrical shock; inside, between the black fabric and the man's skin, was another layer of insulation, this designed to keep the man's body heat in so that he would not register on an infrared detector. Because of this insulation, the interior of the suit was hellishly hot, but the wearer did not complain. Better to be uncomfortable than dead, was his belief.

The night around him was cool and dark. The planet Durward had three small moons, but only one—the smallest—was shining tonight. Its light was scarcely more powerful than a flashlight at a thousand paces—hardly a threat to to give him away.

The house in front of him was another matter. Set out in the open countryside, kilometers away from its nearest neighbor, it looked to his trained eyes like nothing so much as an enormous boobytrap. One false step, one misguided movement would certainly mean the end of his life . . . and possibly worse than that. The fate of the Empire could be resting on his skill, but the thought didn't make him hesitate. There were some risks that *had* to be taken.

There were no guards patrolling the wall that surrounded the house, and that fact worried him more than if there had been a regiment. No guards meant that the wall itself was hazard enough, and that the people behind it expected very few survivors to cross to the interior yard.

Reaching into his belt, the man in black took out a sensitive energy detector and gave the wall a quick scan. He felt no surprise to learn that the barrier was composed of only a thin shell of stone, inside which was a plethora of electronic equipment. The sensors within the wall could detect heat, electromagnetic discharge, pressure, or an attempt to alter the circuit functions. The scattered bodies of birds, insects and small animals at the base of the barrier gave mute testimony to the fate of anything coming in contact with that wall.

The man had come prepared for this eventuality. Beside him on the ground was a long fiberglass pole. Picking it up, he backed off some twenty meters from the wall and then ran at it full tilt. Well-trained leg muscles helped push him upward as he dug the shaft into the ground and pole-vaulted over the barrier. Four meters high the wall went, but he cleared it with easily twenty centimeters to spare.

He hit the ground beyond with his legs coiled under him; he rolled over and used his momentum to propel him into a running start across the open courtyard between the wall and the house. This was a dangerous stretch, for there was no cover but the darkness. He crossed the fifty meters of ground silently, then pulled up panting alongside the building. As far as he knew he was still undetected. He was sweating profusely inside his insulated clothing, but gave not a thought to his discomfort. There were bigger matters demanding his attention.

He walked slowly all around the house, checking the

8

windows. None were open—he hadn't expected them to be—but the alarm system on them was of the standard variety. Reaching into his belt again he took out two wires and clamped them to the edges of the window frame, thus jumping the alarm circuit. With this done, opening the window and slithering inside was a routine matter.

He found himself in an unknown room cluttered with furniture. He dared not bump into anything and make noise; and turning on a light, of course, would have been sheerest folly. Flipping a tiny switch on his belt, he turned on a portable radar device, a type invented for blind people. Instantly, the returning radio echoes painted a picture of the room's layout for him. The door he wanted was three meters away; it would only be a matter of navigating past a few chairs.

Still he didn't move. Reaching again into a belt compartment, he pulled out the sensor he had first used on the wall to check the floor. It was free of electronic gadgetry, so he walked silently across the room to the door.

The portal was also wired with an alarm. He bypassed it the same way he had taken care of the window, opened the door and looked out into the hallway. It, too, was dark, and there were no sounds anywhere along its length. His radar vision informed him that the corridor was free of obstructions, but the scanner indicated that certain planks in the wooden floor were pressure sensitive, and would give him away if he trod upon them. Exercising the greatest of caution, he stepped gingerly out into the hall, moving toward the staircase one agonizingly slow step at a time. Involuntarily, he found himself holding his breath, fearful that even such a slight chest movement would set off the alarms with which this house was booby-trapped.

He reached the stairs and stopped again. According to his informant—a totally reliable one, since he had been incapable of lying under the influence of nitrobarb—the room he sought was on the second floor. Checking out the stairway, he found that a majority of the treads were wired for detection, and that the bannister was carrying enough electrical current to light a small city. The man in black set his jaw determinedly and proceeded to climb the stairs two, three, and sometimes four at a time to avoid stepping on the alarms.

9

"Third door on the right at the top of the stairs," his involuntary informant had told him. Tracing his way around the sensors in the floor, he arrived at the desired door. The handle, his instruments told him, was a bomb that would explode at his touch, blowing him into more pieces than he cared to think about. But there had to be some way of getting into the room and he was going to find it. He scanned the wall and found that it was loaded with electrical circuitry. His eyes read the schematics and discovered that one inconspicuous nailhead in the wall beside the doorsill was really the button that would open the portal.

Still he did not enter immediately. He had been lucky so far in that he had not met up with any living beings. Inside this room, that was bound to change. Human guards would be stationed around the safe night and day, adding extra protection for its invaluable contents. The man in black had no way of knowing *a priori* how many guards there would be; from here on, he would have to rely on luck and his reflexes.

Stun-gun drawn and set on ten—its highest setting—he braced himself for the invasion. The door opened quickly as he pressed the nailhead, a point for him; a slow opening would have alerted the men inside and given them time to prepare for his coming.

As it was, he was almost too slow. There were five guards and two ferocious dogs inside the room. Three of the men were in his direct line of vision and fell instantly as his deadly beams swept across them. The dogs leapt at him from two different directions. He shot the one on his right, but the momentum of its leap carried its dead body crashing into him. Trained athlete that he was, he used that to advantage, falling over backward with the dog's corpse on top of him. His fall caused the second dog's leap to be high, and one of the two surviving guards, who had now had time to draw his blaster, also missed him. The man in black had truer aim; even as he hit the floor, he felled the fourth guard with the beam of his stunner.

The fifth guard also had his weapon out and was using it. But he could not get a clear shot, since his target was covered by the body of the dog. The blaster bolt burned its way uselessly into the already-dead animal, while the invader's reflexes helped him recover quickly. After hitting the floor he rolled to his feet again in one continuous motion, stunner beaming. The fifth guard dropped, as did

10

the second dog. The man in black was now alone in the room with the safe and the valuable piece of parchment it contained.

Speed was what counted now. Though he was almost certain that none of the guards had had the time to set off an alarm, he couldn't afford to bet his life on it. Racing over to the safe, he gave it a quick scan and learned that it was a combination type, wired all over with alarms. The man worked swiftly to neutralize the alarms; when that was done, he used magnetic scanners to guide him through the combination.

When the last tumbler clicked into place, he gripped the handle tightly. Opening the safe would probably set off some sort of alarm, no matter how many he'd disconnected. But that wouldn't matter—once he had the document, the two personal rocket tubes on the back of his belt could take him out the window and away from here before any possible pursuit could be mounted. With a sigh of relief, then, he yanked down on the handle and swung the magnisteel door open.

He had time for just an instant of astonishment as the blaster beam from the ceiling, triggered by the opening of the door, turned his body to a charcoal powder. The charred remains of the expert agent lay in a tidy heap in front of the totally empty safe.

The second man was dressed in robes of crimson satin, the long flowing sleeves of which were edged with three centimeters of white nohar fur—the rarest and most expensive kind in the Galaxy. The satin draped softly over his tall, spare frame, giving him a majestic—if somewhat satanic—appearance. His red satin skull cap, embroidered with gold, clung tightly to his thick mane of black-turning-gray hair.

He turned his head leisurely as the messenger brought him the decoded note, then held the folded piece of paper in his hands for a moment, not even bothering to open it. His long, tapering fingers—which were almost invisible beneath layers of ruby and diamond rings—caressed the smoothness of the paper. He dismissed the messenger and at last opened the missive. The news it contained brought a smile to his sharp features—a smile that would have chilled the heart of anyone observing it. The man unconsciously brought a hand up to his chin to stroke his black goatee as

11

he thought, *That's one more, Zander. You don't have too many left, you know. Then the game will be mine.*

He put the note down on an ornately carved solentawood table beside his chair and picked up the large piece of parchment that had been resting there. In one corner was the colorful achievement containing three gold dragons on a purple background, a bar sinister and thirteen spots on a field of blood. Idly his eyes roamed over the wording of the proclamation beneath the crest:

"Be it known to all people of the Empire . . . Banion is the true son of my flesh . . . Prince of Durward, and all its dominions . . . legitimate heir and successor . . ."

There was no need for him to read the proclamation in detail—he had long since committed the short but important message to his memory. Taking the Patent from its special vault was a dangerous luxury, he knew, but holding it in his hands gave him such a feeling of power that it could warm even the coldest of nights.

This, however, was far from a cold night. No matter what the temperature outside, the news of this SOTE agent's death provided the warm glow of triumph. Handing the Patent to his most trusted vassal to return to its vault, the man in red stood up impatiently.

Time, he thought. *I've waited so long and worked so slowly. I'm not as young as I once was, can I wait until the Plan is finished? Will I live to see that glorious day Mother prophesied?*

This room, lavishly decorated though it was with brocade curtains and silken tapestries, was not soothing enough to the frustrations of his delayed dreams. With long, catlike strides he exited impulsively from the room. He pressed his hand against the secret panel—which was coded to his prints—and a section of the wall slid back to reveal a private elevator tube. A cushion of air solidified under his feet as he stepped in, and dropped him safely and efficiently to a depth of more than fifteen meters below ground level. He left the tube and found himself enveloped by the eerie darkness of the Planning Room.

Walls, ceiling and floor of this room were all black, a total black, a blackness that greedily absorbed all light like some ravening beast. It was a blackness that hurt the eyes to see. But the room itself was not completely dark, for in the center—floor to ceiling—was a sphere seven meters in diameter. Inside the sphere glowed countless thousands

12

of pinpoint lights, scattered seemingly at random—a three-dimensional scale map of human-occupied space. The globe towered over the man's head, an enormous symbol of his vast ambitions.

Blue was the color of Empire, clean and unsullied. Red was the color of his own network. White was unexplored territory, mainly around the edges. Key systems that he controlled were flashing green. There were two yellow dots—Durward, to the top right, and Earth, dead center.

There was still some blue, primarily around the periphery. He dismissed those with a mental wave of his hand. *Mopping up operations,* he thought; *a nuisance rather than an obstacle.* The central core, too, was blue, stretching from Newhope and DesPlaines on one side to improbable Purity on the other. It was a comparatively small volume, and shrinking fast. He came in here at least once a week to check on his progress, and the results were most gratifying. A time-lapse film would have shown a crimson fire devouring the Empire, its tongues of flame licking at the few remaining strongholds.

Soon, the man thought as he stood dwarfed before his towering creation. *Very soon now. Patience will win. And it's your move, Zander.*

The third man was dressed in gray, a conservative suit so nondescript that no one would have looked twice at it—which was the whole idea, since the man's job demanded a maximum of anonymity. He was not an old man by any means, though his bald head and the lines and wrinkles on his face seemed to give evidence to the contrary. His most outstanding feature, though, was his eyes. No amount of outward cover could mask the brilliance that dwelled behind them.

He sat in the middle of his richly-appointed office while around him a building hummed with activity. Computers whirred as programmers typed their input and analysts argued over the results. Clerks moved files from one desk to another, doing their part to keep the river of paperwork flowing dutifully upstream until it reached someone with the authority to make a decision.

Eventually all the paperwork would, in one form or another, cross the large desk of the man in gray, and he would take the responsibility for all decisions. But at the moment, all his attention was riveted on the note that had just been delivered to him by a young, dark-haired girl.

He read the note over three times, not wanting to believe what it said. Finally he looked up at the girl. "Are they *sure*, Helena?" he asked.

"He missed his contact time by a full thirty hours. There's no hard evidence, of course, but we can only suppose that an agent of that caliber would find some way to get in touch in that time—if he were still alive."

"Damn!" The man in gray crumpled the paper into a ball and threw it hard against the nearest wall. His eyes dulled momentarily. "How many does that make?"

"Eighty-nine," the girl said grimly.

The man leaned his elbows on the desk and buried his head in his hands. Eighty-nine men and women that he and his predecessors had sent to their death, all for a piece of paper. One stupid piece of paper that just happened to control the fate of the Empire.

"It's not your fault," the girl comforted. She walked around the desk and put her delicate hands on the man's shoulders. "I don't know all the details of this matter, but it's obviously a lot tougher than anyone ever thought it would be."

"I keep thinking there's something I could have done, some step I should have taken and didn't."

The girl looked at him compassionately. The Service of the Empire did things to a man, changed him and made him more than a mere mortal. Its demands were harsher than a nagging wife. It took everything he had and then dumped him; tormented his failures with guilt and rewarded his success with little more than a nod. But there was always the tradition and the glory . . .

"There's not much you could have done," she said tenderly. "You've used all our best agents."

The man looked up, a far-away expression on his face. "No I haven't. I held the best back, hoping I wouldn't have to use them. Maybe I didn't want to admit that the danger was this severe."

He stood up and paced the room before finally stopping in front of the large picture window. From this height, the vista was magnificent, with waves from the Atlantic Ocean lapping gently against the shores of Miami Beach while the eastern sky darkened with the approach of night. It looked so peaceful that he was almost tempted to disbelieve all the plots that were working against the Empire. Almost.

"I'll admit it now," he said. "I made a mistake. I only hope it isn't too late to correct it." He turned back to face the dark-haired girl. "It's time for the Circus to come to town."

CHAPTER 2

Jules and Yvette

DesPlaines *(Plan)* 15 rev cat 4-1076-9525. Hostile PX-3M-RKQ. Pop (2440) 7,500,000. COL 2018 Fr *(qv)* & NrAm *(qv)* phys. cult. Comml stndg, 229th. Prin ctrib gal: Circus o/t Gal, heav met, prec stones. (Encyclopedia Galactica, *Reel 9, slot 2937.*)

The circus, in one form or another, is one of the oldest forms of respectable entertainment know to mankind. Sporting events, theater, films, radio, television and sensables have all attempted to dislodge it from its status of popularity, with little lasting success. There is still the marvelling at human agility, the gasping at death-defying feats, the suspense of watching people wager their lives on their skills.

The Circus of the Galaxy was just that—*the* Circus. It was the top-drawing show everywhere it played, an attraction whose very name was synonymous with excitement. There were good reasons for the Circus' success, not the least of which was the fact that the Managing Director— who just happened to be Etienne d'Alembert, Duke of DesPlaines—settled for nothing short of perfection in all his acts; and while the Circus remained primarily a d'Alembert effort—fully ninety-eight percent of its personnel were members of that noble family—the d'Alemberts were a clan of considerable talent. At an age when other children were just learning to walk, d'Alemberts were already adept at tumbling. By the time they were five, they were already divided according to their special aptitudes into different branches of the circus that was the family's life and tradition. The d'Alemberts, despite their exalted lineage, took little part in the affairs of nobility. They were *performers*—and more.

16

As usual, the midway and tent were crowded this evening, for this was the first appearance of the Circus on Earth in more than twenty years. Its fame had preceded it, and audiences flocked to it to get a look at what could well be a once-in-a-lifetime experience. The fact that the Circus never allowed its performances to be televised or sensabled entranced the crowds even more.

There were no "freaks" on the midway; the Duke considered such exhibitions degrading and fit only for carnivals, not for the Circus of the Galaxy. But that is not to say that there was not entertainment. There were food booths, where the curious could sample the delicacies of over a thousand different planets. There were games of skill and amusement rides, and over all this activity boomed the voice of Henri d'Alembert, the Duke's nephew twice-removed. "Ladies and gentlemen, nobles and citizens, we present a constantly changing panorama to excite and delight you. Over there in the red booth with the yellow awning is our exotic snack shop. Choose from a menu of over fifty appealing appetizers, two hundred terrific tasty tidbits, five hundred enthralling entrees. All these tender, tantalizing treats await your palate, coming to you from the farthest corners of the Galaxy for prices ranging from a small handful of kopeks to a couple of insignificant rubles. For those not interested in food, we invite you to come watch the wrestling matches about to start in the side tent. See teams of enormous wrestlers vying against one another, testing their strength and skill to the limits. Ride our heart-grabbing Eagle's Drop for thrills you never thought possible. Take your life in your hands and walk through our Haunted House, where there's nothing to fear but the ghosts and goblins." Henri had been chief barker for over ten years; he could—and did—continue his spiel for hours without repeating himself once.

A traveler going down the midway from the main gate to the big tent would pass a gray pavilion marked "Madame Arabella's—Destinies Divined, Futures Foretold." Inside, the beautiful, swarthy-complexioned Arabella would spin tales of the customers' fates using any of the traditional methods, from tarot cards and tea leaves to palms and crystal balls. Whether she had any genuine psychic abilities was still a matter for conjecture, but the fact remained that few of her customers ever asked for refunds.

A few meters further down the midway were the wild

17

animal cages, where the most ferocious beasts from all over the Galaxy were penned when not performing in the center ring. The least exotic of the creatures were the lions and tigers, with which the citizens of Earth were already quite familiar. More unusual were such specimens as the braknel, two meters high at the shoulder with a loud roar and sharper claws; the twin gorjas, a hunting team with fifteen-centimeter-long fangs that injected into their victims the deadliest natural poison known to Man; the liltheran, whose eyes had been known to paralyze its prey with hypnotic effects; the swifter, a beast capable of attaining speeds greater than a hundred and seventy kilometers an hour, and of killing a full-grown great-ox with one swipe of its powerfully muscled talons; and other creatures, less impressive to look at but equally lethal in abilities. Yet this entire array of animal savagery could be controlled by what looked to be a little slip of a DesPlainian girl named Jeanne d'Alembert who, at only age sixteen, was acknowledged as the greatest animal trainer in all the Galaxy.

Closer still to the main tent was the pavilion of Marcel d'Alembert, Illusionist Extraordinaire. One of the most popular attractions of the whole Circus, his act always drew crowds. "You have to watch a magician closely," he told his overflow audience. Holding up one deft hand, he said, "You see this? Well, you should have been watching this one," and from his other hand sprouted a large bouquet of flowers, which he tossed to a pretty girl in the front row. "Misdirection is the key. I tell you to watch one hand and something pops out in the other. Suppose you watch both hands?" He held them up for the audience's inspection, and while their gaze was riveted on his extremities an orange popped out of his mouth. His act continued on in that vein for thirty minutes, with misdirection both subtle and blatant. Even when he told his watchers exactly what he was going to do, they still couldn't see how he did it. But of course, that was to be expected—Marcel d'Alembert was one of the best in the business.

Along the midway, clowns performed continuously. Merry-Andrews, male and female, in outlandish garb and exaggerated makeup played throughout the throngs, taking pratfalls, miming and, in general, managing to be everywhere and do everything wrong. The children laughed at their outrageous stunts, and even the adults found it hard not to discard their masks of urbanity and guffaw with the youngsters.

But all these attractions, as colorful and exciting as they certainly were, were merely *hors d'oeuvres* for the thrilling drama that was now playing inside the enormous, jam-packed main tent.

For twenty-eight minutes, The Flying d'Alemberts—the greatest troupe of aerialists in the entire Empire of Earth for the last two centuries—had held its audience silent. Spellbound. Entranced. For twenty-eight minutes both side rings had been empty and dark. The air over the center ring, from the hard-packed, imitation-sawdust-covered earth floor up to the plastic top forty-five meters above that floor, had been full of flying white-clad forms—singles and pairs and groups doing free head stands on trapezes and sway poles, double trapeze catches, juggling on tightropes, aerial somersaults and other stunts, all utterly breathtaking ... and all without a safety net.

Suddenly, in perfect unison, eighteen of the twenty d'Alemberts then performing swung to their perches, secured their apparatuses, and stood motionless, each with his or her right arm pointing upward at the highest part of the Big Top.

As all those arms pointed up at her, Yvette d'Alembert moved swiftly and gracefully out to the middle of her high wire—and that wire was high indeed, being forty-one meters above the floor of the ring. She carried not even so much as a fan for balance, maintaining her equilibrium by almost imperceptible movements of her hands, feet and body. Reaching the center of the span, she stopped and posed. As far as the audience could tell, she was as motionless as a statue.

Like all the other d'Alemberts, she was dressed in a silver-spangled leotard and tights that clung to every delicious curve of her body, neck to toes, like a second skin. Thus, while she was too short—one hundred and sixty-three centimeters—and too wide and too thick—massing a hefty seventy kilos—to be acceptable as an Earthly fashion model, the sleek lines of her flamboyantly female figure made a very striking and attractive picture—at a distance. Close up, however, that picture changed.

Although her face was lovely enough to tempt any portrait painter, her ankles were much larger than any Earthwoman's should have been. Her wrists were those of

19

a two meter, hundred and ten kilo lumberjack. Her musculature, from toenails to ears to fingertips, would have made any beefcake film or sensable star turn instantly green with envy. For all her weight, she had not a gram of flab anywhere on her body. She looked for all the universe like that incredible Greek ideal of solid womanhood.

After a few seconds of posing—she knew exactly how long she could get away with hamming it—she turned her head and looked down at her brother. Jules d'Alembert, wearing the identical outfit to those of his compatriots, was but ten centimeters taller than his sister, though thirty kilograms heavier. The tightness of his costume accentuated rather than hid the bulges of his powerful muscles. A stone wall would have been soft by comparison, yet his face was handsome enough to melt the hardest of female hearts.

Jules stood on a perch nineteen meters below his sister's level and an "impossible" twenty meters off to one side. The siblings' eyes locked on one another. The audience knew this was to be a feat requiring the utmost in concentration and, as the two d'Alemberts focused all their attentions on themselves, the spectators hushed to a deathly stillness.

Flexing her knees slowly, Yvette began swinging her out-stretched arms horizontally. As the limbs moved in ever-increasing arcs, she put more and more stress into the tautly stretched steel wire beneath her feet.

Jules, meanwhile, reached out his left hand almost casually and grasped a flying ring. His gaze never wavering from the body of his sister so far above him, he began to flex his own knees and move his body in precise synchronization with the swaying motion of the girl-wire system over his head.

The crowd was quiet, frozen with tense anticipation. Yvette's body swayed on its wire, preparatory to her fantastic leap, building ever-increasing increments of momentum. Finally, in the last cycle through which she could hold the wire, Yvette squatted and drove both powerful legs downwards and to her right. But in that ultimate moment, something snapped. The harsh metallic report, loud as a pistol shot, was like a physical blow to the nerves of the audience that had been sitting so anxiously silent.

Several things happened at once:

The wire on which Yvette had stood, no longer being

20

anchored at one end, immediately had all its tension released. Whipping through the air like an infuriated serpent, the thin steel cable dropped toward the ground, coiling in upon itself with loud metallic whinings and slitherings.

Yvette d'Alembert herself, *premiere aerialiste* of the entire Galaxy, was deprived of her push-off spot at the very moment she needed it the most. As her support vanished beneath her, she sprawled helplessly in midair and began her long fall to the ground.

The eighteen d'Alemberts who had been merely watching the trick came instantly to life on their perches. With the reflexes of the skilled acrobats that they were, they seized all the ropes, rings and trapezes within reach and hurled them in the direction of the falling girl, hoping beyond hope that at least one of the pieces would approach within her grasp and save her from a fatal fall.

Yvette flailed out frantically as she tumbled. One of her fingertips barely touched the bar of a swing, and the spectators gasped and dug their fingernails deeper into their armrests. But the trapeze was just out of reach, and none of the other apparatus even came close. Yvette's fall continued unchecked.

Jules d'Alembert was in the lowest position, and consequently had more time to act than did any of the others; but even he didn't have a millisecond to spare. His every iota of concentration had been upon his sister even before the wire snapped, though, so he was mentally prepared to do what had to be done. At the very instant of the break, he pushed himself outward and downward along the arc of the thirty meter radius of his top-hung flying ring. As he flashed through the air, a glittery white blur, it became readily apparent that his aim was true and the force of his launching had been precisely right.

Yvette was falling face down, flat and horizontal, presenting the maximum surface area to the updrafts in an attempt to retard her fall by even so much as a fraction of a second more. As she neared the point of intersection with Jules' arc, her downward speed was greater than twenty-one meters per second. Jules, his body rigidly vertical, was moving almost half that fast as his ring reached the nadir of its prodigious arc.

In the instant before a right-angle collision occurred— a collision that would have smashed any two ordinary athletes into shapeless masses of bloody flesh—two strong right hands smacked together in the practically unbreakable hand-over-wrist grip of the aerialist. At the same time, Yvette did what she could to help her brother with his difficult rescue attempt. Spinning and twisting like a cat—except much faster—she pinioned both her feet against his hard, flat belly. Her hard-sprung knees and powerful leg muscles absorbed most of the momentum of his mass and speed, cushioning the impact his sturdy body would otherwise have had on her. Then, at the last possible instant, her legs went around his waist and locked behind his back. This gave him his right hand free once again, and it flashed upward to join his left in gripping the ring that was all that kept them from seemingly certain death below.

That took care of the horizontal component of the momentum in the two-person system, but the vertical component was worse. Much worse, almost twice as great. Its magnitude pulled at their locked bodies, yanking them downward and into a small but vicious arc. The violent wrenching they received was so savage it would have broken any ordinary man's back in a fraction of a second. But Jules d'Alembert, although only a hundred and seventy-three centimeters in height, had all of his one-hundred-kilo mass in his favor to absorb the enormous strain. The muscles that were barely concealed beneath his leotard were super-hard and super-reactive. His skeleton was composed of dense, strong, king-sized bones, held together by resilient, unbreakable gristle. His arms were as thick as, and immensely stronger than, an ordinary Earthman's legs.

The two bodies were now unstressed relative to one another, but the danger was far from over. They now began to hurtle downward at an angle of thirty degrees from the vertical, toward the edge of the ring facing the reserved-seat and box section of the stands. The people in those sections cringed instinctively and braced themselves for the possible upcoming impact.

Attention now focused on the weakest point in the whole system, namely Jules' grip on that leather-covered steel ring. Could he hold it? Could he *possibly* hold it? Not one person in all that immense audience moved a muscle; not one of them even breathed. Hands clenched involuntarily, trying by some unknown psychic connection to add their comparatively puny strength to that of Jules in order to help him hold on.

The man on the high ring held his grip for just under

half a second; held it while that two-centimeter-thick, super-strength carlon cable stretched more than two meters; held it while the entire supporting framework creaked and groaned under the unaccustomed strain. Then, the merest moment before that frightful fall would have been arrested and both would have been safe, Jules' hands slipped from the ring.

Men gasped. Women—some of them, at least—shrieked. But no one in the audience fainted; a sense of macabre fascination pinned everyone's attention on those two d'Alemberts as they began to fall the remaining twelve meters to the ground.

A high-speed camera, however, would have revealed the fact that their fall was neither haphazard nor out of control. They separated and each curled up into a tight position, knees drawn up to their chins, their bodies braced for impact. As the ground came up to meet them they landed perfectly. Hard-sprung knees took up half of the shock of landing; hard-sprung elbows took half of what was left. Their heads were bent low, with chins tucked tightly against their chests. Powerful leg muscles drove them forward, and thick sturdy shoulders and back muscles struck the floor in perfect rolls. In one fluid, seemingly effortless motion, both brother and sister had hit the floor and somersaulted lightly to their feet.

Hand in hand they posed, motionless for a moment while they recovered their breath. Then they bowed deeply in unison, turned and ran lightly to an exit—and they covered the hundred meters of distance in under eight seconds, at a pace that looked less than a lope.

The multitude of spectators went wild.

They had seen a girl falling to certain death. They had felt a momentary flash of relief—or actually of disappointment?—when it seemed as though her life might be saved. Then they had watched two magnificently alive young people fall, if not to certain death, at least to maiming, crippling injury. Then, in the climactic last split second, the whole terrible accident had become the grand finale of the act.

That it was a grand finale—a crashing smash of a finish —there was no possible doubt. The audience had had its emotions ripped out and wrung for the last drop of feeling. The only question was, which emotion was finally being expressed in that shrieking, yelling, clapping, jeering, cheer-

23

ing, whistling and catcalling throng of Earthpeople—relief, appreciation or disappointment?

No matter; for whatever it was, they had all had the thrill of a lifetime—and few if any of them could understand how it could possibly have been done.

For of the teeming trillions of people inhabiting the thirteen hundred and forty-two other planets of the Empire of Earth, scarcely one in a hundred had ever heard of the planet DesPlaines. Of those who had heard of it, comparatively few knew that its surface gravity was approximately three thousand centimeters per second squared—more than three times that of small, green Earth. And most of those who knew that fact neither knew nor cared that harsh, forbidding, hostile DesPlaines was the home world of the Circus of the Galaxy and of The Family d'Alembert.

CHAPTER 3

The Brawl in the Dunedin Arms

The Service of the Empire (SOTE) was founded in 2239 by Empress Stanley 3, the first of the Great Stanleys, who, during her reign of thirty-seven years (2237-2274), inculcated in it the spirit of loyalty and devotion that has characterized it ever since. Its spirit wavered only once, under the weak and vicious Empress Stanley 5, "Mad Stephanie," whose reign—fortuately very short (2293-2299)—was calamitous in every respect. SOTE came to full power, however, only under Emperor Stanley 10 (reign 2403- -)—the third and greatest of the Great Stanleys to date—under whom it has become the finest organization of its kind ever known. (Baird, A Study of Security, *Ed. 2447, slot 291.)*

The city of Tampeta, Florida, had a population of over fifteen million—a fairly small number compared to Earth's other teeming cities. It included not only what had once been Tampa, St. Petersburg and Clearwater, but also all the other cities and towns between Sarasota on the south and Port Richey on the north. Just outside Tampeta's city limits, well out toward Lakeland, lay the Pinellas Fair Grounds, where the Circus of the Galaxy had been playing to capacity crowds for over a week, with a different show—especially with an entirely different climax—every night.

Jules and Yvette had not even had time to change out of their costumes before they were summoned to the office of their father, the Managing Director. They knew something was brewing, had known it for a month—ever since the Circus had been quickly rerouted here to Earth, breaking more than a dozen engagements in the process.

But nothing had ever been discussed aloud; maybe now they would discover what this was all about.

They gained weight the instant they entered the office, for Duke Etienne kept the ultragrav in this particular room set at a comfortable—for DesPlainians—two and a half gees. The office was well-appointed with springy turquoise-colored carpeting underfoot and richly-grained solentawood paneling on the walls. Three sides of the room were lined with shelves, containing row upon row of books. These were all antiques, since printing was a lost art these days; it was quicker, cheaper and less wasteful of space and resources to store information on electromagnetically-coded reels. Many of the tomes on the Duke's shelves dated back five centuries or more.

The Duke himself was seated behind a gunmetal gray desk, and turned to face the pair as they entered. He was a short man, shorter even than these two children of his, and inclined toward portliness. He was approaching fifty, with hair that was thinning in front and graying at the temples. But time could not dull the glint of life and good spirits that lurked within his eyes even at his most serious moments.

He bid them enter with a wave of his artificial hand. It had been more than a dozen years since he had lost his right hand, severed several centimeters above the wrist by a stray blaster beam; but even that tragic loss could not cripple his indomitable will. His new hand, he insisted, was more than a match for the old one. While it looked and felt perfectly normal to casual inspection, the fingers were really special tools which could be unscrewed just above the knuckle bases and interchanged. Duke Etienne wore rings to disguise the seams, and only his closest associates knew the nature of that artificial member.

He spoke bluntly to the two aerialists, without preliminaries, in the Franco-English *patois* that served as the native language of DesPlaines. "This is it."

They both knew instantly what he meant. The moment they had really been training themselves for all these years had arrived. For just a moment they were speechless, then Yvette blurted out, "What's the assignment?"

"I don't know." The Duke shrugged his shoulders, a gargantuan gesture of uncertainty. "They didn't see fit to tell me that. I'm an old man now, perhaps they don't trust me any more." But though his words were resigned, there was a twinkle in his eyes that softened their impact. "All I know is a place and a code signal. Oh, and I have this to give you." He reached into his desk and pulled out a plastic microfile card.

"What is it?" Jules asked, taking the proffered card from his father's hand.

"The Head's retinal pattern," Duke Etienne said off-handedly. "You may need it to make a positive ID. I'd suggest you don't lose it."

Brother and sister stared at each other in astonishment. The Head's retinal pattern! That little plastic card would be worth a large fortune to enemies of the Crown. The fact that they were being given this meant that they would actually be meeting that illustrious personage—and *that* meant that this job was going to be more important than they could possibly have imagined.

The Duke then told them the recognition code and where they were to make their contact. "I'd suggest you go camouflaged," he said. "We DesPlainians are a little too overly-muscled to pass unnoticed on Earth."

The two younger people thought for a second, then Yvette said, "How about going as Delfians? They always wear those long, heavy robes and never take them off in public. We'd still be noticed in that get-up, but in a different way."

The Duke nodded appreciatively. "Splendid. Misdirection, as Marcel would say. I'll call right down to Wardrobe and have them get the costumes ready for you." His tone indicated that he thought the discussion should draw to a close. As the two younger d'Alemberts stood up to depart, he looked them both squarely in the eyes. "Take extra care, both of you, and good luck. Oh, and take the good car." They knew which one he meant.

Both of them raced down to the Wardrobe Department, where Mimi—one of their great-aunts—outfitted them perfectly: Yvette in a pale blue Delfian robe and hood, Jules in silver. They were so excited at the prospect of this new action that they could say nothing.

Thus it was that two short, heavy-set Delfians, muffled to the eyes in the shapelessly billowing robes and hoods that were the trademarks of their planet, milled through the crowd that was still departing the main tent and even yet talking about the unbelievable act it had witnessed. It took half an hour for the crowd of people to file through

27

the exits and out into the enormous parking lot, but those mysterious, silent Delfians appeared to take no notice of time. Delfians, as everyone knows, are never in a hurry.

They found the car at the far end of the lot. At first glance it appeared to be a standard sports model Frascati, a low, sleek, silver-gray bullet for shooting down the highway. Only to the trained eye would that car have appeared a little too long, a little too wide, a little too round and much too heavy to be a standard model—and, of course, there was a reason for that.

Once out of the traffic jam created by cars leaving the Fair Grounds, Jules maneuvered his sporty vehicle up into the second level, westbound stretch of Interstate Four. Like all cars on the more civilized planets, this one was equipped with the option of being computer-controlled by the electronic guidance equipment installed in the roadbed itself, but Jules preferred to do his own driving—and his reflexes were almost as fast as the traffic computer's.

It took almost no time at all to reach the Dunedin district and pull into the parking lot of the Dunedin Arms, one of the most exotic nightspots along the renowned Gulf Strip. At the Arms, Jules slipped a twenty ruble bill to the parking lot attendant—the car could have been parked automatically, but Earth had to find *some* jobs for its surplus billions—another to the resplendently-uniformed doorman, and a third in the palm of the usher who escorted them, with great ceremony and a flourishing of his arms, into the elevator tube and up to the dining room on the fourth floor.

No one thought it unusual that the two Delfians refused to part with any of their mufflings, for such was the custom of their secretive race. Jules did, however, tip the cloakroom girl a five ruble bill just for being clad in, as Yvette put it later, "a couple of sequins and a bangle." The two Delfians, alas, had no reservations, but a fifty ruble bill slipped to the table captain brought beneficent assurances that something would be ready for them shortly. "Thank you, gospodin and gospozha," the maitre d' said obsequiously. "There will be a delay of perhaps five minutes, regrettably, but not more than that. Perhaps you would care to spend that time having a cocktail in our bar?"

The table captain had spoken in Empirese, the Russo-English mixture that was the official language of the Empire, and Jules answered in the same tongue. "That would be delightful, thank you." This delay was included in his plans.

The entrance to the bar was just in front of them. Jules and Yvette paused at the threshold and gazed around the huge room. The decor was dark, elegant, subdued. At the right, running the entire two hundred meter length of the room, was the bar, made of ornately-carved rare mahogany and backed by a mirror that was veined and flecked with gold. The far wall was a rich chocolate wandwood, hung with heavy velvet draperies of dark red. Little niches were spaced every few meters along the wall, in which resided suits of armor and marble religious statues from ancient medieval times. Wrought-iron sconces held myriads of candles; their light mingled with the candles set in the three enormous wrought-iron chandeliers to illuminate the room to a comfortable, if not bright, degree.

On the left were three tremendous windows overlooking the beach and the open Gulf four floors below. On a stage at the far end of the room, a pair of entertainers from one of the more exotic planets—perhaps Binhalla, judging from their long, slender appearance—were engaged in a sleek, sensual dance depicting a mating ritual and leaving little to the imagination. For the most part, the audience—which was seated at the sturdy solentawood tables scattered not too closely spaced around the floor—gave the dancers their full attention, with the exception of several parties engaged in private conversations. The room was jammed with a bright, colorful and festive crowd, all thoroughly enjoying themselves; there were only a few vacant spaces at that incredibly long bar.

"Yes indeed," Jules reiterated, taking his sister's arm. "A cocktail or two would be sublime."

At the bar, Jules laid a fifty ruble bill on the surface and said, "Two vodnak slings, please. Made with Estvan's from a new bottle; sealed, if you have it."

"We have it, gospodin." The barkeep seemed slightly insulted that they would question his integrity as he set before them the heavy, crudely-molded green glass bottle of the one hundred and twenty proof beverage that was the favorite tipple of the rim-world, Delf. "We've got just about everything. The Dunedin Arms caters to all tastes."

Jules was just as glad his face was muffled as he gazed at the distinctive bottle that was the unmistakable trademark of Estvan's, for with the hood and wrappings the bartender would not see the grimace he made. DesPlaines' dense atmosphere had, over the centuries, wrought subtle changes in the body chemistry of its inhabitants, making them allergic to alcoholic beverages in any form. Though he and Yvette could drink the cocktails—and would in the line of duty—the sensation would be unpleasant and he was not looking forward to it.

The bartender broke the seal on the bottle and poured the glasses about three-quarters full of the vodnak, then added the dashes of jumberry fizz that made vodnak slings such popular drinks. Taking the fifty ruble bill from the countertop, he brought out ten rubles and assorted kopeks change. Jules waved the money away with an impatient gesture.

"I do believe," he said, holding his glass up to the light, "that this is the only civilized drink in all the Galaxy." His voice was loud enough to be heard for several tables away.

"In all the Universe!" Yvette chimed in, just as loudly.

Neither of them had the opportunity to taste their beverages, though, for within several seconds a tall, slim Earthman had come up to the bar, taking the spot next to Yvette. He did not look at the ersatz Delfians, but instead held up one finger to attract the bartender's attention. When that worthy came over to him, the newcomer began, "I'll take a jigger of the . . ."

That, however, was as far as he got. Yvette, whose eyes had remained constantly on the mirror in front of her, detected a rapid movement down at the near end of the bar. Rapid as that motion was, though, Yvette's reaction was faster. Reflexes on a planet like DesPlaines, where even a simple stumble could shatter bones, tended to be lightning fast.

The old-time circus battle-cry of "Hey Rube!" had survived even to this day—at least in part—so that her shout of "Rube!" brought her brother, as well as herself, into instant action. She grabbed the heavy Estvan's bottle that the bartender had resealed, gripped it firmly by its neck and hurled it even as she dropped. A vicious blaster beam blazed through the air, incinerating the slender Earthman and sweeping through the space her chest had occupied just an instant before. Still in air, falling almost flat, she braced one foot against the bar and pushed off it as strongly

30

as her powerful thighs could manage. Her drive brought her head-first under the nearest table; bending her back, she heaved it upward.

But the deadly blaster beam she feared had already died out—along with the gunman who'd fired it. The heavy bottle, made of thick glass and half-filled, had been hurled with a DesPlainian's strength and with an aerialist's sure control. It had struck bottom-on squarely in the middle of the gunner's face—and now that gunner had no face at all, and scarcely enough head to be recognizable as human.

Jules had not been idle during this interval, either. He, too, had dropped at his sister's warning, scanning the room as he fell. But he hit the floor like a spring, with his legs tight under him. In what looked to be a contradiction in action, he fell to the ground and leaped simultaneously. His leap was high and far, toward a table for six three meters away at which only two couples sat. One of the men at that table, half hidden behind a tall, statuesque blonde, had begun to rise to his feet and was reaching for an object inside his overtunic that made just the slightest bulge near the left armpit.

Jules lit flat on the table and slid angle-wise across its length. His terrific momentum carried him—along with a welter of breaking and flying dishes, glassware, silverware, food and drink—directly at the man trying so frantically to draw his weapon. En route, Jules stuck out one arm and brushed the blonde aside. He didn't push her hard at all—just a gentle, one-handed shove, enough to get her out of the way. Nevertheless, she went over backward, chair and all, performing an involuntary somersault that sent her skirt flying to reveal a stun-gun hidden on the inside of her thigh. She landed on her head and was knocked instantly unconscious.

Continuing his slide, Jules made a point of his left elbow and rammed it into the man's gut. Then, as the man doubled up and *whooshed* in agony, Jules whirled off the table to a standing posture and chopped the hard, calloused edge of his right hand down on the back of his victim's neck. The snap of that neck breaking was audible ten meters away above the uproar and screams then going on.

As the man dropped lifelessly to the ground Jules, in one deft motion, snatched the man's half-drawn weapon and glanced at it. It was a stun-gun rather than a blaster, but its dial was set at ten. Wide open. Instantly lethal. That,

31

Jules decided, would never do, so he clicked it back to three—a half hour stun. Then he played its nerve-jangling beam briefly over the other couple at the table—who had appeared far too unconcerned during all this action to be truly unconcerned—and whirled around to see how well his sister was making out.

Yvette was doing quite well. The table under which she had disappeared had leaped into the air, turned over—shedding glasses far and wide along the way—and crashed down at the end of the bar where the first blasterman and three other goons had been standing. Yvette was right behind it, a fury on wheels. The loose, flowing Delfian robes were only a minor encumbrance as she moved, a factor that she had to take into account. One quick swoop sufficed to pick up the fallen blaster, which she then tried to bend around the side of the second man's head. The gun broke up almost as thoroughly as the head did.

The third man had now had time to reach for his own blaster. He had no compunctions at all against using it in so crowded a room; any number of innocent people could die as long as he wiped out the two targets. The beam had, in fact, already incinerated three patrons at the bar before Yvette could take effective action. Ducking as only someone with her reflexes could, she grabbed this third man by the ankles, up-ended him and kicked the flaming blaster out of his hand before it could do any more damage. As she rolled to her feet once more, she lifted the thug up over her head and was about to use him as a flail on the fourth when that unlucky wight slumped bonelessly to the floor under the beam of her brother's stunner.

She had the motion all made, though, and acrobats frown on wasted motion. So, continuing her swing, she hammer-threw the man she'd picked up over a few rows of tables and out into fifteen meters of air through the middle of one of the three immense windows.

Have you ever heard forty-one square meters of one-centimeter-thick plate glass shatter all at once? It makes a noise.

Such a noise that all lesser noises stopped instantly.

And in that strained, tense silence, Jules spoke quietly to his sister. Both were apparently calm, neither breathing so much as a single count faster than normal. Only their eyes —his a glacially cold gray, hers a furiously hot blue—

32

betrayed how angry and disconcerted they both were. "Many more of them, you think?" he asked.

"Not to spot." Yvette shook her head. "And we've got no time to check."

"Right. Take that one, I'll bring the other. Flit." Carrying the two unconscious men who were left alive, the d'Alemberts ran lightly, but at a terrific speed, down three flights of stairs and out into the parking lot. The attendant was startled to see the two wealthy Delfians who had entered the building so recently running out now carrying two very dead-looking human bodies; he tried simultaneously to run and to yell, but accomplished neither—a half hour stun from Jules' gun saw to that.

Loping across the darkened parking lot, they spotted their car and reached it in seconds. They dumped their reluctant guests in the aft compartment, then climbed in themselves and slammed the doors shut. Tortured rubber shrieked and smoked as the heavy car spun out of the lot and onto the highway. Fortunately the traffic at half past two in the morning was so light that Jules didn't have to drive far before a moment came when no other car was in sight.

There was a reason why the d'Alembert vehicle was a little longer, wider, rounder—and much heavier—than a standard car. Now, alone in the road for a moment, Jules punched three innocent-looking studs on the control panel, and three things happened: 1) the car's lights went out; 2) the two halves of an airtight, beamproof, transparent canopy shot up from those too-round sides, snapped together, and locked; and 3) the vehicle went straight up into the air, at an acceleration of four Earthly gravities—they didn't dare hurry with two Earthers aboard—to an altitude of sixty kilometers before it stopped.

Their Delfian disguises had come through the action pretty much the worse for wear. Jules and Yvette removed the tattered remnants and stared wordlessly into each other's eyes for a long half minute. Then Yvette spoke.

"That was our contact—our only contact. And we don't know anybody in SOTE on Earth."

"We could go back to Father," Jules suggested. "If he could arrange this meeting there must be ways to set up others."

Yvette shook her head. "But this meeting was *blown!* There was a leak. There *had* to be a leak, Julie."

33

"I'm afraid you're right. And it was no ordinary leak, either—it had to be right in the Head's own office . . ." Jules' voice died away.

Yvette shivered. "Any meeting Father could set up might get blown the same way—and next time, we might not be lucky enough to get away. Any ideas?"

"Only one. We've got to find the Head ourselves."

"We've got his retinal pattern," Yvette conceded. "But aside from that we haven't an inkling of who or where the Head is. He may not even be on Earth."

"Well, there's bound to be somebody here in the Tampeta office, and they'll be on the alert. That brawl put the stuff into the fan but good. They'll be monitoring the channel every second, waiting for us to make our move."

"But our friends' friends down there will be monitoring *all* channels every second—and they probably have the codes if they were able to know about our rendezvous."

Jules thought for a minute, then grinned. "So I'll go back to one that's so old and so simple that they probably never heard of it—unless it'd fool our monitor, too."

"I don't think they'd have any mental defectives manning the SOTE boards at a time like this," his sister commented.

"True. *Alors,* here goes."

He flipped a blue switch and raised his powerful—and not painfully unmusical—deep bass voice in song: "Sing of the evening star, Oh, Susan; sweetest old tune ever sung. Oh, Susan, sweet one, 'tis everything soft, Oh . . ."

"Susan here." A lilting, smooth-as-cream contralto voice came from the speaker. There was a moment of silence, then the voice said, "Cut!" and Jules flipped his switch once more. Satisfied, the voice concluded, "We'll beep you in. Out."

"I'll say they're alert," Yvette commented. She half-giggled in relief, then went on, "And she's fast on the uptake—'Susan here' my left eyeball. You made that whole thing up on the spur of the moment, didn't you?"

"Uh-huh. If I'd had a little time the verse would have been as good as the music."

Yvette snorted. "Ha! Modesty, thy name is Jules! Perhaps you should have gone into opera instead of acrobatics. But we were right about one thing, at least—no mental defective could have made 'S-O-T-E—S-O-S' so fast out of *that* mess of yowling. But my guess is it won't really be a beeper."

"Anything else but. I'd bet on a laser. They've got us lined up and they'll pour it right into our cup—so I'd better set the cup spinning."

He did so, and in less than a minute the pencil-thin beam came in, chopped up into evenly-spaced dashes by the rotation of the cup-antenna of the car. There was, of course, no voice or signal.

While Jules was lining up his finders to determine the exact line of the beam, he said, "Better unlimber the launchers, Evie, and break out some bombs. Just in case somebody wants to argue with us on the way in. I'll handle the other stuff."

"That's a thought . . ." She broke off, and her tone changed. "But just suppose that's *their* beam?"

"Could be; so we'll have to look out even more carefully when we land. But they know that. So if everything's smooth they'll engineer a safe approach—we won't have to. They know who we are—I hope."

His words were optimistic, but his tone was grim. Things had gone fatally wrong tonight. They had given the right signal at the rendezvous—but the wrong people had responded. Now they had to find out why!

CHAPTER 4

The Head

Democracy as practiced in the twentieth century failed because it could not cope with the dynamic tyranny of the Communist powers. This failure had its roots firmly anchored by the end of the third decade of that century and, though there was a period in the sixties and seventies when détente looked promising, the deteriorating world situation with regard to population and ecology brought the failure into focus. Even the formation of the North American League— comprising Canada, the United States of America and Mexico—on the eve of the twenty-first century could not stop democracy's decline. The Congress of the N. A. L. argued and filibustered, but could not agree on any effective action to contain the enemy that was rapidly devouring the so-called Third World of developing nations. The Russo-Chinese War, which had at first looked like a boon to the democratic powers, actually served to strengthen the Soviet Union, honing their skills and whetting their appetites for bigger game. With no other rivals to his ideological leadership, the Premier of Russia could act. He issued orders, the recipients of which either obeyed them or were promptly shot. (vanMees, History of Civilization, Reel 21, slot 1077.)

The laser beam that was to guide them in was weak, indicating that it was coming from a considerable distance away. While Yvette stood guard against any possible sneak attacks, Jules fiddled with the control panel to convert their "car" into an atomic-powered jet capable of speeds up to a thousand kilometers an hour. As they burned their way through the atmosphere, heading southeast, the male d'Alembert kept a close watch on his ultra-sensitive radar screens to avoid any other aircraft.

"I wonder where we're going," Yvette said after a few minutes of flight.

"Well, it can't be more than four hundred and fifty kilometers away, or they wouldn't be able to reach us with a straight-line laser beam. Our bearing indicates Miami— there's nothing beyond that in this direction but ocean."

"Headquarters could be on a floating platform or in some undersea base," Yvette speculated. "Or it could be in some isolated spot between here and Miami."

"Possibly. We'll just have to wait a few minutes more to find out."

But as the minutes passed it became more and more apparent to them that Miami was indeed their goal. For twenty minutes they slid down the beam, slowly losing altitude as they did so. The half-hour stun Jules had given their two passengers would be wearing off shortly, and he was considering giving them an extra short jolt when their target came into view. Slowing down to gain maneuverability, the d'Alemberts looked the site over.

The building was enormous, at least ninety stories high and towering over its closest rival by almost forty floors. Bright floodlights at the base kept the lower half of the structure constantly lit as bright as daylight and, even though this was an extremely late hour of the night, more than half the windows in the broad side of the building were lit. The silhouettes of people working could be seen passing by many of the open windows.

"Impressive place," Yvette commented.

"Scan it before we go in. I'd like to know where we're headed." He pulled the car to a stop while they were still a kilometer away from the building, and there they hovered for several seconds while Yvette completed her check.

Switching on her special sensing equipment, she scrutinized the building from top to bottom. "The place is armed like a fortress. Big guns, probably capable of knocking out a cruiser, but they're all well hidden. They're all warm, but none of them are fully energized at the moment."

Jules considered that. "That doesn't tell us any more than we could have guessed by ourselves. Headquarters would certainly be armed that way; the enemy camp might be, as well. How about visual? What building is that, anyway?"

Yvette switched easily to a magnified TV picture. "Hall of State, Sector Four. That would make sense. Four has always been the most loyal sector, and State would be the best place to hide the Service."

"Check. Where's our beam coming from?"

"Rooftop. There's a small broadcaster located in a circle of light. I see one human figure standing in the circle, and infra shows one other person standing in the darkness outside that ring."

"What do you think?"

"I'd risk it," Yvette said without hesitation.

"We've got no choice, really." Jules stroked his chin. "We have no other leads, nowhere else to go but home. *Alors,* in we go. Just keep your hand on the launchers, in case."

Jules approached gingerly, heading for that spot of light on the roof. As they came nearer, the figure standing in the light grew more distinct. It was a girl, young and skinny— though not too bad looking for an Earther, Jules thought. She had long black hair that fell halfway down her back, and was wearing a beige sweaterdress and brown tights. She had a throat-mike around her neck—and two heavy-duty Mark Twenty-Nine Service blasters in her hands.

After dropping the car to within two hundred meters, Jules stopped and hovered in the air over the girl's head and waited for her to make the next move. When she saw that he was coming no closer, her highly distinctive, throaty contralto voice came again from the speaker. "It's safe to talk now if we don't say too much. Are you armed?"

"Yes." Jules, as per her suggestion, was not saying too much.

"Good. You won't need these, then." The girl walked out into the very center of the ring of light, put the brutal hand weapons down on the roof and stepped back to her former position. In essence, she was disarming herself and putting herself at their mercy—a gesture they would have appreciated were it not for the person on the roof who, according to their sensors, was still in the darkness.

"You recognize my voice, of course," the girl went on.

"Yes." Jules was getting by on as little conversation as possible. Yvette kept silent; so far, only Jules' voice had been broadcast. It might be of some advantage if potential enemies thought there was only one person in the car.

"I suppose you have a retinascope," the girl went on.

"Yes. Hold on a minute." He switched off the com and turned to his sister. "What do you think of this?"

"They want us to identify someone by retinal pattern. But the only person we have a comparison disk on is the Head himself. If they're the genuine article, they'll know that."

"Which means that either the girl or her friend in the shadows *is* the Head—and *that* means we'll have to rough up our boss a bit before we can establish his identity."

Yvette bit her lip. "Well, they have to convince us about themselves one way or another, and that would do it. Besides, what else can we do?"

"Nothing," Jules agreed, and again flipped the blue switch. "Go ahead. What do you suggest?"

"Land anywhere you please and one person will come aboard. Unarmed."

"*Khorosho,* will do." Jules dropped down outside of the illuminated circle and, stun-gun in hand, opened the port on his sister's side.

The person who had been standing in the shadow approached slowly. All that could be seen of him in the darkness as he came near with empty hands outstretched was that he was a man of medium height, medium build, and that he was almost completely bald. He put his hands in through the port and Yvette, taking one of his wrists in each hand, helped him through the narrow opening. The front compartment of the car was now quite cramped, so the d'Alemberts weren't too worried about violence from this gentle-looking man. Nevertheless, Yvette held him securely, his arms behind his back, while Jules applied the retinascope to the Earthman's right eye.

Jules took a long time comparing the actual eye pattern to the one recorded on the card his father had given him. But there could be no mistake—they were identical. Almost reverentially he whispered, "The Head himself. I'm sorry, sir . . ."

At Jules' acknowledgement of the man's identity, Yvette immediately released her hold on him and offered a similar apology. The Head stretched his arms to limber them up again in the narrow confines of the front compartment, then laughed deeply as he said, "Think nothing of it. If you'd acted any differently you wouldn't have been the right people for the job. As it is, Jules, I'm very glad indeed to meet you in the flesh," and the two men shook hands vigorously—with Jules being careful not to squeeze too hard, for fear of shattering his boss's hand.

"And you too, Yvette, my dear," the Head continued. Taking her hand, he kissed it in as courtly a fashion as if that tiny, cramped compartment were the Imperial Ballroom itself. "And now—purely a formality, of course—the eyes. Yvette first, please," and he handed her the retina-scope.

She was a little surprised as she fitted the device to her eye. "But you didn't put any disk in," she said. "Surely, sir, you don't . . ."

"I surely do." He studied her pattern briefly, then switched the 'scope over to her brother and studied his. "I don't know very many patterns, of course; but Jules and Yvette d'Alembert? You're too modest altogether, my dear."

"But . . . but why should you bother to memorize our patterns?" Yvette continued to protest. "We haven't really ever done anything for you yet, just a couple of small assignments."

"As has been said of acting, there are no small assignments, only small performers. Jules, of course, is the only living person to achieve a perfect score on the thousand point test—and Yvette, your nine ninety-nine was, shall we say, exceptional?" The test to which he referred was one administered to all SOTE agents during their training. It tested logical capacity, physical agility, reflexes, intuition and a host of other subtle qualities needed by a good agent.

"It's true," he continued, "that I haven't given you any major assignments so far, for much the same reason that you don't use cannons to kill mosquitos." His face clouded over. "Perhaps I waited too long to get you involved in this case, hoping it could be solved by lesser means." Then the cloud vanished as he forced himself into a better mood. "But you're both here now, and perhaps you'll end up wishing you'd stayed strictly with the Circus."

He reached over and flipped the blue switch for the com unit. "Still safe out there, Helena?" he asked the girl, who had not moved from the circle of light.

"Still safe, Father," the girl radioed back, and began to walk toward the car. "Nothing suspicious, Detection tells me, within five hundred kilometers of here."

"Fine," Jules said, opening the door for them to get out of their cramped quarters. "I was hoping we were fast enough to get away smooth, but I couldn't be sure. Now, sir, about our guests," and he jerked a thumb toward the rear compartment where the prisoners were sleeping off the effects of Jules' stunner.

"Ah, yes. I've been wondering about them. The reports were confused and contradictory."

"I'm not surprised; it happened pretty fast. That one," Jules pointed, "is probably only a low-bred beambat who doesn't know a thing. The other one may not know anything or he may know a lot, it's hard to tell." He related, in a very few words, about the too-imperturbable observer of the brawl. He finished: "So our secret rendezvous was no secret."

The Head's face looked grim. "I see." He raised his left wrist to his lips, and the d'Alemberts could see that he wore an ultraminiaturized com unit strapped on there. "Colonel Grandon."

"Yes, sir?" came the prompt response.

"Be on the roof in exactly two minutes. You'll find two men who received number three stunbeams about twenty-five minutes ago. They're in the rear compartment of a Mark Forty-One Service Special near Space Jay Twelve. Revive them, find out what they know and report."

"Very well, sir."

The Head led the way over to an elevator tube. "Come along," he said. "I don't want anyone but Helena and me to see you two. Your identities are—I hope—still secret, and I'd like to keep it that way." Jules and Yvette followed their boss to the tube, with the girl named Helena coming after them.

Cushions of air materialized under their feet and dropped them down to the thirty-first floor, where a door opened in front of them and they entered what was very obviously the private office of an exceedingly important man.

The room was fairly large, furnished richly but quietly. The entire eastern wall was a large picture window, looking down upon the sleeping city of Miami and out beyond to the dark blot that was the Atlantic Ocean. The brown rug was thick and luxurious, while the beamed ceiling was of beautifully grained brown solentawood and the paneled walls were of the same fine, almost metal-hard wood. Original oil paintings by some of the most noted artists of the day adorned those walls, except for the one behind the large solentawood desk. On that wall was inlaid the gold-crowned Shield of Empire, its double-headed eagle gleaming even in the subdued indirect lighting.

The Head went immediately to his desk and turned a dial. Gold curtains swept soundlessly into place, covering the picture window. Jules and Yvette guessed—correctly—that the Head didn't want to take any chances of having telephoto pictures taken of this pair of his top operatives.

"Now we can talk," said the girl behind them. Then, holding out her hand to Jules, said, "I'm Duchess . . . Oh, excuse that, please!" She flushed hotly as Jules knelt to kiss her hand in true Court style. Standing there with a red face until he finished, she then proceeded to shake hands cordially with both Jules and Yvette.

"She should blush, friends," the Head said, but with no more than mild reproof in his voice. "But she hasn't been in the Service very long." Turning to the girl, he went on, "Outside titles mean little in here. You are merely the Head's Girl Friday, my dear. Our guests are of the thinnest upper crust of the entire Service; their worth to the Crown is immeasurable—far beyond any number of duchessess. We'll sit down now, please, and Helena will pour. She knows my usual." He cocked an eyebrow at his two agents. "Yours?"

"Orange juice, please," Yvette said promptly, and Jules chimed in with, "Lemonade, please, if you have it handy."

Helena cast them a quizzical glance, which the Head noted with a smile. "Our guests are from DesPlaines," he he told her. "Their bodies don't tolerate alcohol very well."

Helena pursed her mouth into a small *oh* and proceeded to mix the requested beverages. The one she poured for herself looked like some sort of cream liqueur. When the glasses were distributed, the four people sat back in their chairs to discuss their current problem.

"The attack on you two was a complete surprise," the Head said in a quiet voice. "No leak, nothing irregular was even suspected until the man who was to bring you here to me was killed. The connection between this business and the matter that brought you to Earth is clear. In that context, it's a highly pleasing thought that the opposition knows nothing of you or of the Circus. You agree?"

"I agree, sir," Jules said, and Yvette nodded her concurrence.

But Helena was puzzled. "How can it follow that they don't know, Father?"

42

"The d'Alemberts are new to you because there is no record anywhere of any connection between them and us. The Circus has been SOTE's primary weapon ever since the Service's formation, but no record of that fact has ever been written down. Except for this surprise attack, even you would not be learning all the details now. I'll go into more detail after they leave, but for the present I'll simply state as a fact that no one who knows anything about them would send only eight people against Jules and Yvette d'Alembert. Or, if only eight, all eight would have fired simultaneously at them and on sight, instead of burning the contact man first. That shows that they were more afraid of the Service here than of the supposed Delfian agents—a fatal error."

"Oh, I see—excuse me, please, for interrupting."

"That's quite all right. It's part of your education, Girl Friday."

"But even if they didn't know exactly about us," Yvette pointed out, "they did know that something was supposed to happen. There *was* a leak and we have to plug it—fast."

"Right," Jules said. "Who knew about the meeting?"

The Head began checking them off on his fingers. "There's me; I rule out that possibility. There's the two of you; you weren't too likely to set yourselves up to be killed. There's your father, the Duke; if he wanted to kill you, he could have done it at the Circus and made it look like an accident, without tipping his hand in this clumsy a manner. There's Sarbatte, the agent who was to contact you; I suppose he's a possibility, even though they killed him. He might have told them about the meeting thinking they would just kill you, and they decided to kill him too to make it look good. It's unlikely, but possible."

"What about her?" Jules calmly pointed at Helena with the hand holding his glass.

The Girl Friday blushed and shook her head. Her father took the accusation in stride. "Not possible. She knew that the Circus was somehow involved, but I never told her about either you or the meeting. I only enlisted her help the instant we heard about the mini-riot at the Dunedin Arms, because I knew I could trust her."

"Anyone else know?" Yvette prodded.

The Head frowned. "Sarbatte's superior, Colonel Grandon. He's the chief of our entire Internal Security division. I wanted the building on alert just in case the opposition tried something."

"Isn't he the one you sent up to the roof to pick up our two prisoners?" Jules asked.

The entire scene froze as each of the four people in that room realized what might be happening. Decisively, the Head stabbed out a finger and activated a TV monitor on his desk. An adjustment of a dial brought an infrared view of the rooftop onto the screen.

There were now two cars on the roof. A man—it could only be Colonel Grandon—was dragging an unconscious body from the d'Alembert vehicle to the other. "Grandon!" the Head barked into a microphone. "Put that body down and report to my office immediately."

Grandon jumped as the Head's voice blared out at him from speakers on the rooftop. He looked around wildly for a moment; then, realizing he was still alone but being watched, he panicked. Moving quickly, he hauled the unconscious assassin over to the edge of the roof and pushed him out into air. Then, without waiting to watch the man fall ninety-three floors to his death, he ran back to his car and fled at top speed.

CHAPTER 5

The Chase

Even before Oliver Fenton Arnold invented the subether drive that made galactic exploration possible, all of Earth except the N.A.L. was under Communism —and North America itself was being infiltrated and undermined. The real explosion of mankind into space, however, did not begin until 2013, when John Copeland discovered the uranium-rich planet Urania Four, thus assuring all mankind of cheap and virtually unlimited power. In 2016 the American anti-Communists, disgusted and alarmed by the success of the "do-nothings" and "do-gooders" in blocking all effective action, left Earth en masse for the promising— and aptly named—planet, Newhope. Whereupon Communism took control of all Earth without firing a shot or launching a missile. (vanMees, History of Civilization, Reel 21, slot 1281.)

The d'Alemberts had not waited to see what Colonel Grandon's reaction to being discovered would be. Even as the Head was reaching for the button that turned on the rooftop speakers, their lightning reflexes had catapulted them out of their chairs and into instant action. Their common thought was to get up to the roof as quickly as they could and stop this traitor before he could do any more damage. Both of them raced across the room to the elevator tube, which they reached simultaneously.

The air cushions materialized as expected under their feet, but the ride up the tube seemed interminable. Indeed, it was nearly a minute and a half before the lift brought them to their destination—a timespan impossibly long to people who were used to measuring their movements in milliseconds.

Colonel Grandon had taken off in his own car by the time Jules and Yvette burst out of the elevator doorway. As they rushed across the open rooftop to their own vehicle, though, they heard a telltale *whoosh* directly over their heads. "Split!" Yvette shouted, and they did—just as a blaster beam from the airborne car burned a trail directly through the spots where they'd been. The searing ray scorched the edges of Jules' clothing just a trifle as he dove forward, rolled, and got back onto his feet in one continuous motion. He never stopped running.

Colonel Grandon hesitated a moment longer above them, wondering whether to try another shot to kill—or at least delay—his pursuers. But then he realized that every second counted. Each instant he spent in target practice would mean that much more time the Head would have to mobilize the forces of SOTE—and Colonel Grandon knew precisely how vast those forces were. He would need every nanosecond to effect his escape.

While he took off into the darkness of night, Yvette and Jules scrambled across the flat roof to their car. It took them a full fifteen seconds to reach it, another five to jump in and close the doors, five seconds to start the engines, and five more to convert the craft to aerial flight. Thirty seconds in all, and another thirty added on because Grandon's vehicle had gotten a flying start. The traitor was a full minute ahead of them.

With Jules in control, the d'Alembert car shot off the edge of the roof, accelerating as it went. Yvette was watching the sensors, trying to pick up a reading of the fugitive. "Got him!" she cried at last. "Bearing twenty-six degrees northwest and running like a swifter with its tail on fire. We'll have a hell of a time catching him."

Jules grunted as he brought the craft up into the higher levels of atmosphere, so that there would be less air resistance to impair their speed. There wasn't any planetbound vehicle faster than a Mark Forty-One Service Special—but Colonel Grandon had one, just as they did. All things being equal, the two cars should maintain their twenty kilometer gap until one or the other of them ran out of fuel.

"Why doesn't headquarters fire on him?" Yvette wondered. "They've got enough firepower to down a battleship."

"They're not shooting for the same reason we won't," Jules said. "We have to get Grandon alive. Killing him won't incapacitate the people he's working for—we have to assume he's already told them everything he knows. On the other hand, we'd like to know some of his secrets, like who he's working for. Killing him would lose us some valuable information."

"Then we'll have one advantage in this chase," Yvette said. "His own side isn't going to help him against us. I was a little worried they might come to his rescue."

But the d'Alemberts were not the only ones capable of reasoning this way. Apparently, Colonel Grandon too knew that he was expendable to his side, and that he was on his own. He had to keep his distance from his pursuers; if it looked as though they were gaining on him, he was pretty sure his allies would step in and shoot him down to prevent what little he knew from falling into SOTE hands.

Therefore, while the SOTE agents behind him had to hold their fire, he did not. Putting the guidance controls on automatic, he locked his craft into its course and turned his attention to the vessel behind him. It stubbornly kept on his tail, even though the people in it must have known they would not be able to catch up to him. He would have to do something to discourage them.

The one man he had been able to rescue from the back of the other car was beginning to come around, but the effects of even a mild stunner dosage took some time to wear off. Grandon knew the fellow would be too groggy for the next hour or so to be able to help much with the fighting. He grimaced at the realization of exactly how alone in this he was.

Taking aim at the car behind him, Grandon fired off the multiblasters that made up such a deadly part of his car's armament. As he'd expected, those fearsome weapons had little effect on his pursuers, whose beamproof shields were as tough as his own. He had hoped that whoever was in that car would waste some time trying to dodge the beams, but they apparently knew the capabilities of their vehicle too well. They flew straight at him, without shifting course in the slightest.

Okay, Grandon thought, setting his chin, *we start to play rough.* The flick of a lever brought his launchers into play, and the press of a button loaded them with bombs.

In the following vehicle, Yvette gasped as her scanners showed the bomb that had been lobbed out the rear of the

47

fugitive car. While it had been aimed roughly at them, there was not a chance that it could have spanned the almost twenty kilometers between the vehicles. Instead, the bomb would miss them and fall on the densely-populated land below, killing thousands—perhaps millions—of innocent people.

Instantly her trained reflexes came to the fore. Aiming up her own multiblasters, she fired them at the falling projectile. As the deadly beams scored a direct hit, the bomb exploded in midair, sending a shower of small and relatively harmless debris down upon the countryside. Jules, meanwhile, kept their car flying straight after Grandon's, so there was no slackening of the chase.

Now, however, the fugitive was making matters more difficult for them. He launched two bombs straight downward, in widely scattered directions. Cursing under his breath as he saw them fall, Jules brought the car into a slight dip to give his sister a better shot. The female d'Alembert picked off these two projectiles with the same uncanny accuracy, but by the time Jules could bring the car back up into pursuit they had lost two more seconds of valuable time.

Again the traitor's vehicle shot out bombs endangering innocent lives, and again the d'Alemberts reacted to protect the people of Earth. This time there were four of the bombs, and they were dropping so fast that it took a full ten seconds to blow them out of the sky and return to their flight path. "We'll never catch him at this rate," Yvette cried.

"Oh, I think the Head still has a few tricks up his sleeve," Jules replied. "Look there."

He pointed at the scanner and Yvette looked in the indicated direction. There, at the extreme left edge of the screen, was a swarm of bright little shapes moving eastward. Their path would just about intersect that of the traitor's car. "Tampeta division," Yvette guessed.

"Right, they'll try to cut him off and turn him back. If he should somehow make it by them, there'll be other fleets just waiting for him. The Head probably has every flyable vessel in North America in the air right now, hovering on alert and waiting for developments to break. Nobody, not even Grandon, could wiggle out of a cordon like that."

Even though the odds were now against their capturing

the runaway colonel themselves, the d'Alemberts continued to watch the developments playing out on their screens. Grandon had spotted the Tampeta fleet as soon as Jules did, and was now in the process of taking evasive action. His own car was smaller and more maneuverable than most of the SOTE craft in that formation, and he used that fact to masterly advantage. The fugitive dipped and soared through the atmosphere on an unpredictable roller coaster that kept his pursuers guessing. His flight path veered sharply off the northwesterly course it had been following and began moving straight north. This, of course, invalidated the intersection course of the fleet and caused them to readjust their direction; after which, Grandon veered again. He was counting on the maneuverability of his craft to help him skirt around the approaching fleet, flank them and outdistance them.

It almost worked.

Just over Jacksonville, Grandon encountered another blip—a commercial airliner on its regular route down to Miami. The treacherous colonel had dipped very low into the atmosphere in an evasive maneuver when suddenly the plane appeared out of nowhere, coming at him almost head on. He banked quickly, and just did miss hitting the plane, but his reflex action cost him dearly. At that speed, and with his air resistance at that altitude, his car lost control. Buffeted now and helpless in the face of a series of crosswinds, the car shook and trembled. Down he plummeted, and the lower he went the less control he had.

With his vehicle that out of control, the d'Alemberts were able to gain on him. Grandon's car was still too far away to be visible in the darkness of the early morning, but their scanners told them the story. The fall would be fatal, they could tell that; it had already gone too far to ever come under control, and they were still too far away to make any attempt to save it. Jules and Yvette could only watch helplessly as the final catastrophe hit.

With a blinding and deafening crash, Grandon's car plunged headfirst into a suburban park. Only by the most fortunate of coincidences did it miss impacting in a residential neighborhood, and consequently no innocent human life was lost. But the vehicle itself made a pretty scene. Special Service cars like that one were never meant to be inspected by the general public, and were equipped with self-destruct mechanisms. As the vehicle smashed to earth, it turned into an enormous fireball that illuminated the landscape for kilometers around with a light brighter than a dozen suns. The sound of that tremendous explosion shattered windows within a ten block radius, and the shock-wave could be felt halfway across the city. Nothing remained of the car and its contents but a fine dust that rained down on the city of Jacksonville for more than six hours afterward.

Colonel Grandon did not get to become the chief of SOTE's Internal Security division by being stupid. When his vehicle began to slip from his control after the close brush with the airliner, he knew instantly that this present situation was hopeless. Being a man who could act quickly on reflexes, he moved at once to improve his chances of survival.

Consequently, at the very instant his car was being volatilized on impact with the ground, Colonel Grandon was floating suspended in air by a parachute, one kilometer above ground level. He was reasonably certain he would not be spotted. At nighttime he would not be a visual attraction to anyone's eye—and to pick him up on an infra-red scanner, an observer would have to know precisely where to look for him. That was unlikely. So, as he drifted leisurely down to earth, he had time to think about what to do next.

His car was gone, and with it the man he'd tried to save from SOTE's probings, probably under nitrobarb. He did not regret his action—that man, had he been forced to reveal what he knew, could have given SOTE a clear enough description of Grandon to blow the colonel's cover anyway. But, with the destruction of the car, he would probably also lose his pursuit. There was no possibility of any body surviving in the wreckage, so they would have no anybody surviving in the wreckage, so they would have no lay out a search pattern for him just on the possibility that he had eluded destruction, but of necessity that search would have to be a general one. With nine billion people currently inhabiting the surface of the planet Earth, any man who knew what he was doing could easily avoid detection by that type of search.

He landed in a residential section. His chute was of a specially designed material and vaporized at the touch of a match, leaving virtually no trace of its existence. He walked for several blocks to the nearest subway entrance, and took the first available train to anywhere. He changed trains three times at random before finally going to his destination—the monoliner station. At the ticket counter he bought a pass to Angeles-Diego, but used the passenger option and converted it once he was aboard the train to the Boswash Complex.

The Atlantic Seaboard from Massachusetts to Virginia was jammed with a population of more than a hundred million souls. Within that seething mass of humanity, of fleshpots and rampant confusion, a highly trained professional like Colonel Grandon easily avoided all the nets that had been cast for him. Twenty-four hours after arriving in Boswash, the fugitive had safely boarded the first in a series of airliners to relay him to his real destination—Moscow.

Twelve hours later, he was proceeding through channels to report to the man who'd paid him to betray the SOTE. A call to the proper number was relayed up the chain of command; and after a delay of only one hour—which indicated an efficient organization—his instructions came back: he was to go to a certain address and report to whomever he found there.

The house was an old one, a decrepit building on the seamier side of town. The windows were all boarded up and the bricks were grimy from decades of air pollution. There seemed to be no decent people on the streets—only what the colonel would have classified as "the criminal element"—though many people looked at him through drawn shutters. The bannister of the outside stairs was covered with dust, undisturbed for months. This house was not a frequently visited spot.

Inside, the house was not much better. The smell of old cobwebs assailed his nostrils, the walls were covered with faded old wallpaper and the floor was bare except for an old board or two scattered about the floor. Grandon reached for a light switch, but nothing happened when he flipped it. The only light available was that which managed to filter in through the boarded up windows.

"Hello," he called out.

"Over here, Gospodin Jones," came a muffled voice from behind one wall, calling him by the prearranged code name.

Grandon took a step toward the voice. "Your Majesty, I . . ."

"Do not come any closer." The voice coming from the next room was still muffled, but sharp. "You will stay at all times where I can see you and you cannot see me. It is a necessary precaution. And you are not to refer to me by that title—yet. I will not claim what I have not earned. It will come, in its season. Meanwhile, you will call me Gospodin Ivanov. It is not my name, but it will serve."

"As you wish, gospodin. I've come to you to report firsthand on the moves SOTE is making against you."

"The very fact that you are here at all—firsthand or otherwise—is indication that you have failed me. I paid you to be *inside* SOTE."

"That couldn't be helped. Your other agents botched the job. I provided them with enough information to lay a perfect ambush. They failed. The fact that two of them were captured compromised my position. They didn't know me by face or name, but there would be no doubt about where their information had come from. I knew I would be of no use to you dead or, worse, subjected to nitrobarb, so I escaped. The Head currently has no idea of where I am—or, in fact, any more than the merest suspicion that I'm still alive."

"What have you learned about his immediate plans? In particular, who is this secret agent he's called in?"

"I can't say, but it does seem to be a team. Sarbatte, the agent who was to rendezvous with them at the Dunedin Arms, was told distinctly that there would be two of them. As I was escaping from the building I saw two figures following me. I shot at them, but apparently missed; I was in a hurry, you understand. It was dark up there, and I couldn't make out more than two shapes, so I can't tell you any more than that."

"You have failed me, Gospodin Jones," the voice reiterated. "These supposed superagents are still alive, and their identity is still unknown."

"But I can make it up to you," Grandon said desperately. "I know the workings of SOTE inside and out; that knowledge is invaluable."

"Yes, I've read your reports; they were quite thorough. SOTE trains its people well. I wish my own people could report as concisely and accurately as you."

Grandon smiled.

"In fact," the voice continued, "your reports were so

start; they still felt guilty about his escape. They had let the Head down.

Their boss could read the dejection in their eyes as they reentered his office via the elevator tube. He had already received verbal reports from the fleet commander about Grandon's fate, and had set in motion the necessary search machinery just in case the colonel had not died in that crash. There was nothing more to be done about that situation, and he resolved not to dwell on it.

"I was aware that we had some problem with a leak," he said slowly, "but I hadn't realized it was that high up. Now I'll have to stop almost all work while we regroup and recheck for loyalties. But in the meantime, we'll have to continue on with the business I had in mind for you. The fact that there *was* so high a leak indicates how important it was that we send for the Circus—and particularly for you two."

"Yes, you might as well tell us," Yvette sighed, trying to overcome her depression. "We've been ambushed and shot at, and chased a traitor all the way across this peninsula. It would help to know what it's all about."

As his sister spoke, Jules could feel a pair of eyes watching him. Looking over to the corner of the room, he saw Helena gazing his way with a dreamy sort of look on her face. As their eyes met, she smiled warmly at him. Jules hastily turned his attention back to his boss.

The Head nodded at what Yvette had said. "As you can see, there's trouble. It's centered, we think, on the planet Durward. There are forty-odd reels of records concerning our investigation, which I'll give you before you leave; but there are also a number of things that aren't on the record and never will be. That's why I wanted to discuss this with you in person. The investigation will be entirely in your hands, and you'll be free to conduct it in any way you wish. You may want to question some outsiders to get the full picture, and you may want to conduct a preliminary examination on Earth or elsewhere before you go anywhere near Durward."

The Head stood up and, out of habit, walked over to the window where the drapes were drawn. His back was to his daughter and the d'Alemberts. These two DesPlainians were potentially his most valuable agents, and the fact that he had brought them here was a measure of the importance he attached to the situation. He had fully expected some sort of trouble waiting for them between the Circus and his office . . . and he'd been equally confident that the d'Alemberts could handle it.

But, he had to force himself to admit, they were still unproven. True, they came from the most able of bloodlines, and were members of a family that had served the Empire well almost since the inception of SOTE itself. True, they had trained for their job practically since birth and, as tests showed, they could do their work more capably than anyone else in all of human-occupied space.

The question still remained: had he waited too long to summon them? Had he let his own pride in his ability to handle the situation delay matters too long? Could even the d'Alemberts deal with the menace that threatened the Empire now?

He turned back abruptly to face the other three people in the office. "Let's fill in some background. For example, consider the question of loyalty. The Service is totally loyal to the Crown as the symbol of the Empire. The wearer of the Crown, whoever he or she may be, is the very focal point of the Empire. You agree?"

"Of course, sir," Jules said. The two girls just nodded.

"Very well. In early 2378, when Crown Prince Ansel was planning the murder of the entire rest of the Royal Family, if we had caught him at it in time we of the Service—I speak in the first person, even though it was long before any of us was born—we would have burned him down, Crown Prince though he was, because he threatened the Crown itself."

"Why, I . . . suppose that . . . yes, sir," Jules said.

"I never thought of it before in just that way, sir," Yvette added. "But that's the way it would have to be."

"Of course. Ansel himself recognized that principle when, after accomplishing his coup, he executed the Head of the Service for incompetence in letting it happen. Nevertheless, those eleven murders did take place, and Ansel, as the sole surviving member of the House of Stanley, became Emperor Stanley Nine. Was there then any question of punishment for his deed, any thought of gunning him down? No. We instantly became as loyal to him as we had been to his father, Stanley Eight, and now are to his son, Stanley Ten. We are the Service of the *Empire*, not of any one particular emperor. Whoever sits on that throne *is* the Empire."

"Of course, sir. But what . . . ?"

"Now comes some off-the-record material. Have you ever heard of Banion the Bastard?"

Jules thought for a moment. "I don't think so, sir," he said. Yvette also shook her head.

But this time Helena began to nod ever so slightly, and said, "Oh, oh—a light beginneth to dawn."

Ignoring his daughter, the Head went on, "I didn't think you two had. The whole affair took place a good many years ago, and has been hushed up quite well since then. Not too many people now alive would remember the name. But, in point of fact, that name is the crux of our problem today."

He went back to his desk, sat down and took a sip of his drink, collecting his thoughts and wondering how best to phrase the history lesson. "Stanley Nine's weakness was women, particularly young ones. Even before he ascended the Throne so abruptly, his love life had been speculated upon in the scandal sheets—and had he not been next in line of succession there were even juicier stories that could not have been squelched. By the end of 2378, just a few months after assuming the Crown, he had gotten married —and to a very beautiful, intelligent girl, I might add. No matter; her hold on him was never any more permanent than that of innumerable others, both before and after. By the middle of 2379, Empress Odina was of as little importance to Stanley Nine's life as the drapes in the Imperial Ballroom. He visited her occasionally to try to produce a legitimate heir, but otherwise she was almost a ghost in the Imperial Palace."

"Poor woman," Yvette sighed softly.

"Yes, quite so. Meanwhile, with the Emperor on the loose again, as it were, others saw their chance to profit from his weakness. In particular there was one Henry Blount, Duke of Durward. He was thirty years old at the time—just four years senior to the Emperor—and a bachelor, and eager for power. He saw in Stanley Nine's womanizing a chance to influence the Throne itself. If he could just place the right woman in the Emperor's bed, he would have Stanley Nine's ear and shape his policy. But not just any girl would do; the woman who would be the Imperial courtesan must have very special talents.

"Duke Henry scoured his entire planet, and of course

57

found the perfect woman for his plans. Her name was Aimée Amorat . . ."

"The Beast of Durward," Helena interrupted, looking over at the d'Alemberts with a special eye toward Jules. "Surely you've heard of *her*."

Neither Jules nor Yvette had.

"You must remember, my dear," her father said gently, "that court scandals are kept alive on Earth a great deal longer than they are on the farther planets, merely because this is where they occur. As the size of the Empire increases, our internal communication becomes fuzzy, and . . . but this isn't meant to be a lecture on imperial logistics, so let me continue with my story.

"Gospozha Amorat was precisely the woman Duke Henry was looking for. She was young—twenty-two, I believe—and had beauty enough for three woman, according to the legends. She was extremely intelligent. She was an aspiring actress so that, while being sexually experienced enough to cater to the Emperor's tastes, she could act coyly enough to cater to his fantasies. And, one of the primary points in her favor, she had not a scruple to her name. She was as cold-blooded, vicious and hard as Duke Henry himself. She well earned her nickname.

"She and Henry quickly came to terms and set their plots in motion. He brought her here to Earth and financed a tremendous social debut at the next Grand Imperial Court. Of course she was unknown, which in itself made her intriguing to the young Emperor. Once she turned her charms on him, he never had a chance—and when she sank her claws in, they were there to stay.

"With Duke Henry's full backing and her own considerable guile, she managed to keep Stanley Nine on the hook longer than any other woman was ever able to. Their romance was the talk of the court for five months before an even more important topic supplanted it—the Beast was pregnant with the Emperor's child.

"Stanley Nine had had illegitimate children before; you could populate a planet with his less-than-legal offspring. Normally, the mothers were just given a stipend and sent along their merry way—but Aimée Amorat was not one to be dismissed so lightly. She had turned the Emperor's head so far that rumors of divorce were actually flying through the Court. Fortunately, as I mentioned, the Empress Odina was a pretty smart woman herself. The vast

58

majority of the Court was on her side—they all hated the usurper from Durward—and she rallied her support and persuaded Stanley Nine to keep her. But even with this play foiled, Duke Henry and the Beast were not entirely out of the picture.

"When Aimée was about seven months' pregnant, the Duke married her—with Nine's full approval. Thus her son, Banion, was born in wedlock as the first child of—and the direct heir of—the Duke and Duchess of Durward. That wasn't enough for the schemers, however. Stanley Nine was still blindly infatuated with the extremely talented Beast and, at her insistence, issued a Patent of Royalty, admitting his paternity and bestowing upon the infant the unique title of 'The Prince of Durward.' This Patent also authorized a coat of arms as follows:

" 'Purpure, quarterly three dragons rampant or, in chief sinister a bend sinister or, in dexter . . .' "

"Wait up, Father!" Helena broke in. "You're not getting through to me at all, and I don't believe that's our guests' language, either."

The Head laughed. "Excuse me—I sometimes forget that heraldry isn't for everybody. Basically, it's gold dragons rearing on purple enamel. The bar sinister, which need not be a mark of illegitimacy, in this case definitely was. It goes on that way for a couple of hundred words, only a few of which are pertinent. 'Bordure gules, charged thirteen bezants sable.' Poor heraldry, really—color on color and an unlucky number of spots on a background of blood—but that and the fact that the Patent was dated Friday the thirteenth of June, 2380, are perfectly in keeping with the Duke's vicious sense of humor.

"Things went on this way for three more months, until suddenly the Duke's plots came crashing unexpectedly down around his head. Empress Odina was pregnant, and there would be a legitimate heir to the throne.

"All at once, Stanley Nine came to his senses. Here was a man who had wiped out the rest of his Royal Family just to attain the Throne, and yet he himself had been foolish enough to establish a pretender to the Crown with a perfectly valid claim. The taste of that must have been pretty bitter. He could not, of course, allow that Patent to stand. He ordered the Service to kill the Duke and Banion, and to destroy the Patent; but he was far too late. One of Duke Henry's spies at court had already informed him of the

Empress's pregnancy, and the Duke and Duchess realized immediately what that meant. By the time the Service could act, they had disappeared completely—*with* the Patent.

"The Patent, of course, was the most important thing. It was handwritten and signed by Emperor Stanley Nine himself, on Imperial parchment, with the signature driven into the parchment by the Great Seal of the Empire of Earth. The Patent was revoked and erased from all record; the people involved were proscribed; but that wasn't enough. The actual physical document had to be found and destroyed—but it wasn't. Banion the Bastard had to be found and killed—but he wasn't.

"Those are the crucial facts, though there were a few developments since then. With their success gone, the Duke and the Beast quarreled. Apparently she tried to lead a rebellion against him; her hope was to kill him, renounce the Patent and try to get back into the Emperor's good graces. But her coup failed, and she barely escaped with three vital things: her life, her son and the Patent. There has been no official trace of any of them since.

"Duke Henry, on the other hand, was captured in 2383. He was questioned quite severely about the location of the Patent and the child. He genuinely didn't know their whereabouts, and so Stanley Nine had to settle for executing the Duke for treason."

The Head paused and let out a deep breath. "In the meantime, the search that started sixty-seven years ago is continuing. It began in 2380, twenty years before I was born. As I said, the record of it covers more than forty reels. Results have been nearly nil, except for three very good forgeries, yet somehow this lack of results has cost the Service eighty-nine lives." He paused again, to let it sink in. "Eighty-nine. A hideous waste—and the number has been accelerating of late. Two year ago, several leads came to light, pointing back to Durward. We sent in some good agents to investigate. Three months ago, all those agents stopped reporting. Then I sent in three more, of a much higher caliber, and gave them orders to avoid all previous contacts. They disappeared without a trace. I sent in one more just three weeks ago, one of my absolute best. Vanished; he was gone as though he never existed."

He pounded a fist down on his desk in frustration. "Damn it, there is something out there that is eating my agents, and I don't like it. We must find out what it is and stop it, before it grows completely out of bounds. That's why I brought in the Circus, and particularly you two; you're the heaviest artillery the Service has. The threat to Stanley Ten and the Royal Family is grave indeed; just how grave even I didn't comprehend until the events of tonight, with the attack on you in the bar and the discovery of Colonel Grandon's treachery."

The Head stood up, walked over to where Jules and Yvette were seated and stood in front of them. "Most of the principals in that story are dead. Stanley Nine and Duke Henry most assuredly are—we have adequate proof of that. Aimée Amorat would have to be ninety years old if she is still alive, so we can tentatively rule her out as a viable force. The Bastard, though, at sixty-seven could still be kicking up a lot of traces—and I won't even begin to speculate about his possible children and grandchildren, of whom we would know nothing."

He placed a hand on the shoulder of each d'Alembert. "I may be overstating the obvious, but I can't stress enough the importance of this mission to the succession. Stanley Ten was the only legitimate heir to Stanley Nine, and he in turn has only one heir, his daughter. If anything should happen to them, the Galaxy could be plunged into chaos. The Bastard or his heir would undoubtedly come forward with the Patent to make his claim—and it would be the best one, under the circumstances. The Patent would —and probably does, to judge from Grandon's case— play havoc with the Service's loyalties by confusing people about whom to support. Not to mention a lot of hitherto loyal dukes and grand dukes who might decide to dispute that claim in their own favor if given half a chance. The result would be civil war, one which could last for centuries and cost untold billions of lives. Our entire civilization could collapse under that heavy burden. It's a thought I hate to contemplate, yet I must—because I, and you also, have the responsibility of preventing it."

The Head straightened up again, placing his hands at his sides. "The Service's prime duty, of course, is to protect the Emperor and, after him, his successor. Until tonight I'd thought we could accomplish at least that safely enough; now I can't be certain just how riddled our organization is with traitors. Whoever has the Patent has been patient, so far, building his opposition to us with meticulous care until he's wormed his way right into our vital organs. We can't expect him to wait much longer before he makes his final bid for power."

"Our mission, then," said Yvette, "is to destroy the Patent and whoever is holding it."

"Not exactly," the Head said. "It's a little more ticklish than that. You must find the genuine Patent, to be sure, but we also must have it brought intact, so that Stanley Ten can destroy it with his own hands. Only then will the Throne be safe. Also, you must find Banion the Bastard and capture him alive, if possible; he's built an organization that is threatening the Empire and, if we're to destroy it, we'll need his intimate knowledge of how it works."

Helena was still looking at Jules with that warmly disconcerting gaze. He ignored it, stood up and looked directly into the Head's face. "You'll have our best effort, sir, I assure you."

The older man smiled. "Then I'm satisfied. I have the utmost confidence in you two." He handed them a box containing the records they would need to check, then led them back to the elevator tube. Helena came over and unexpectedly kissed Jules goodbye. The DesPlainian blushed as he and his sister stepped into the tube.

"Goodbye and good luck," the Head called after them— adding, under his breath, "We'll all need it."

CHAPTER 7

Citizens of Earth

In two centuries, the colonized planets numbered seven hundred, many of them having large populations. As improvements were made in the subether drive, interstellar commerce and communication increased exponentially. And, as usually follows such a trend, interstellar crime increased as well. The colonies still held a sentimental attachment for their mother planet; in fact, Earth had been acting as an unacknowledged imperium for years. After the Koslov and the short-lived Gomez dynasties died out, the Stanleys ascended the throne, providing Earth with strong and able kings. Finally, in 2225, King Stanley the Sixth of Earth decided to claim in title what was already his in fact, and crowned himself Emperor Stanley One of the Empire of Earth. (Stanhope, Elements of Empire, Reel 2, slot 39.)

With no need to hurry, now, the d'Alemberts drove their car back to Tampeta via surface highways at a leisurely one hundred kilometers an hour. For a long time, both were silent; the import of what the Head told them had had a very sobering effect, and the responsibility he'd placed on their shoulders was weighty. The fact that, in their first major assignment, the fate of the Galaxy was at stake frightened them.

Finally, to break the silence, Jules said, "I knew the Head would have to be a high muckamuck, but I never guessed *how* high. If his unmarried daughter's a duchess, he can't be anything less than a grand duke. I think maybe I've seen his picture somewhere, or seen him in a parade or something on tri-dee . . ."

"Oh, *brother!*" Yvette snorted. "And I use the term advisedly. You're the thousand pointer, how come you didn't recognize Grand Duke Zander von Wilmenhorst on sight? Oh no, he isn't much of anybody—just one-half Stanley blood and fifth in line for the Throne itself, is all. You'd better break out your Peerage and start studying it."

Jules banged the side of his head with his palm as though to clear it. "I must be dense today. But what a cover for the Head of the Service! He *owns* Sector Four!"

"If you play your cards right, you could own it next." Yvette's voice was dipped in sarcasm. "I saw the way that girl Helena was ogling you. All you'd have to do is marry her and you'll be in line to be a grand duke yourself."

Jules blushed hotly. "I did nothing to encourage her, And besides, I'm already engaged."

"I know that and you know that, but someone neglected to tell Helena."

Jules let the subject drop there and drove along in silence.

They arrived back at the Circus shortly after sunup. Even now there was some activity—a big show like the Circus of the Galaxy never sleeps—but they knew that their father would not be awake until later in the day; and besides, they themselves were exhausted. They had lived through more excitement in the past twelve hours than even the super-human body was built to withstand. So, instead of reporting in immediately, they grabbed a quick snack at the commissary, then went to their quarters and slept for ten consecutive hours. Then, relaxed and refreshed, they went to visit their father.

The Duke sat impassively as they related their adventures with the ambush in the Dunedin Arms and of their first meeting with the Head. He scowled when he heard about the traitor who had wormed his way so high up in the Service echelon. When they had finished telling about the chase, a silence followed. "Well," the Duke asked, "what's your assignment about?"

The two younger people fidgeted and looked at one another. The Head *had* told them that most of the briefing was off the record and, even though he hadn't given them explicit instructions about secrecy, he'd no doubt assumed that they would use their discretion. Even though their father was a duke and a top SOTE agent himself, he had no real need-to-know. The fewer people who had knowledge of their mission, the safer they would be.

The Duke saw their hesitation and laughed. "Can't even tell your poor papa, eh? Don't be embarrassed about it. I've known so many secrets in my life that knowing one less certainly won't kill me. I'm very proud of you both today, *mes enfants*. An assignment this crucial means you are finally ready to take your place in the universe, a place that's awaited you since birth. I may worry a little about your safety, at times, but not too much. You know what you're doing—last night proved that. I've taught you all I know; now's the chance for you to use it.

"But," he continued sadly, folding his hands in his lap, "this of course means that you will have to leave the Circus, your home for nearly thirty years."

"I know," Yvette saild softly. "That's the thing we've dreaded most."

"It's one thing to face danger," Jules agreed, "and quite another to leave such good family and friends behind."

"It is necessary," their father shrugged. "All growth requires changes and sacrifices of something, I suppose. Fortunately, the break need not be total or permanent; you will be cherished, but not missed." He stopped, and looked up at them. "*Alors*, what are you waiting for? Get out of my office before I start to cry and ruin my whole day."

Yvette came over to him, kissed him on the cheek and whispered, "*Mon bon papa*," in his ear. Then the two top agents in the entire Galaxy walked out of the office.

They did not leave the Circus just yet, though. By unspoken agreement they stayed around until the evening performance, where they melted into the crowd of Earthers who jammed the arena to see the show. As part of the audience they watched, with trained and minutely observant eyes, as Yvette and Jules d'Alembert flawlessly performed a heart-stopping variation of the act they themselves had performed only the night before. Then, with the performance over, they went down to the commissary to congratulate their younger "selves."

The new Jules and Yvette, still in their spangled outfits, sat down boisterously at the table with the older pair. The two men looked very much alike, as did the two women— unsurprising, in view of the fact that they were chosen, among other things, for their appearance. The younger models were their cousins, twin children of Marcel d'Alembert, the Duke's younger brother. They were ten years junior to the older pair, but only a DesPlainian could have

65

spotted the age differences. As for the minute differences in facial appearance, few people outside the Circus would know. Jules and Yvette d'Alembert were never photographed close-up, and never appeared on tri-dee or sensables. All the audience ever saw of them was their flashing forms flying through the air, performing seemingly impossible acrobatics. Only now, those flying forms would be unnoticeably different.

This succession of top stars was routine to the personnel of the Circus of the Galaxy. In the two-hundred-year history of the Circus, there had been more than a score of pairs called "Jules and Yvette d'Alembert"; and, as long as the d'Alembert clan and the Circus held out, there would continue to be a new pair every decade. The pair now retiring had gotten their own start when their predecessors died on a mission for SOTE twelve years ago, and hence began their careers prematurely. The new pair would have a quiet and unexciting changeover.

"How'd we do, *Grand-père?*" asked the younger Jules. This was his first public performance in the starring role, and the thrill of the applause was still racing through his bloodstream. "It must have been a treat to see a good performance of your act."

"Close the orifice, Jules," his partner broke in.

"Oh, you're calling me 'Jules' already, then?"

"Certainly," said the younger Yvette. "You *are* Jules, now, while he goes on to be a nameless shadow serving the Empire. But what I started to say was, that's the way people break their arms, patting themselves on the back so much."

"*Khorosho.* What I meant was, I'm glad the Head pulled them out of the Circus for special duty. It wouldn't be too long before they'd splattered themselves all over the ring, the way their joints are creaking now. How *about* that, Jules?" and Jules II grinned at Jules I.

"That is true and very sad, Jules," Jules I agreed as a waitress came up to take their orders. "Yvette and I got this cushy assignment just in time. The ancient and unwieldy bones are just about ready for the fertilizer mill. The old-time pep is all shot . . ."

"Dear Jules, you're breaking my heart," said the waitress, dripping with sarcasm. She, of course, was a d'Alembert, too, and had been one of the supporting aerialists twenty-five years ago, when Duke Etienne had been a

66

performer with the Circus. Even when the talent to perform was gone, the d'Alembert clan never let any of its members want for employment. "Stop crying before I lose all control and dilute your soup with a flood of my own tears. The King and Queen are dead, et cetera. So what? You're just getting started on your real jobs. The usual?"

"Not quite," Yvette I said. "You can get fresh orange juice here and I'm drowning myself in it. Squeeze me half a liter please, Felice dear, besides the usual."

" 'Drowning yourself' is right," the younger Yvette said darkly. "I've got to watch my figure; I'll settle for one small glass of lemon sour and a lamb chop."

"That's the thing about performing," said the older Jules. "Appearance is everything. Now that we're 'retired,' Yvette and I can eat to please ourselves." Yet his actions belied his words as he ordered a very modest meal. All the d'Alemberts were extremely conscious of the health value of their food.

After eating their late night snack, the older Jules and Yvette bid farewell to their family and left the Circus—without leaving so much as a ripple to let the outside world know they'd gone.

Driving eastward across the darkened highways for several hours, the pair arrived at the Cape Canaveral Spaceport, the interstellar terminal that serviced the southeastern portion of the North American continent. The journey was uneventful, and at last they arrived at the field. They snugged their car down into its berth in the belly of their own ultra-fast, two person subspacer, *La Comète Cuivré*—The Copper Comet. This vessel, a sleek dart built for speed and power, had been a gift to them from their father two years earlier, in anticipation of the day they'd become full-fledged agents and need transportation of their own. Its burnished form was indeed a spectacle in daylight, gleaming under the bright Florida morning sun.

They spent the next two days living aboard their ship as it sat on the ground. They studied, analyzed and reviewed forty-seven reels of top-secret data, then sent them —through the most devious of routes—back to the Head. They drew charts based on the information they'd read, made statistical analyses, tried to find patterns in the confusing and conflicting facts that would point them in the right direction.

With that accomplished, and some tentative hypotheses reached, they consulted with the Head again. Headway was being made but slowly in weeding out potential traitors to the Service, for the simple reason that they couldn't let the people know they were being weeded. A spy you know can be an asset, as long as his side doesn't know he's been spotted. So far, three potential traitors—out of the thousands of people working for SOTE on Earth—had been uncovered and were being watched. But there were other signs that all was not well within the Empire.

Crime was flourishing on the Mother Planet. True, a certain amount was to be expected on a world with a population of nine billion, but the situation was much worse than should be anticipated. Criminals were much better organized here, and their hold on the populace was far too tenacious for chance. While the Service was not responsible for dealing with ordinary crime per se, it maintained files on what was going on—and the reports that were filtering up to the Head's office were deliberately vague and misleading. It was as though someone, at some level, were trying to cover up the true extent of the problem. Estimates of harmful effects were almost unanimously understated, as though to lull the upper echelon into a false sense of security. Until now, those tactics had worked all too well.

To Jules and Yvette d'Alembert, the situation shrieked for action—and instant, effective action at that. If the Service caught a chill, hundreds of outlying planets faced the threat of double pneumonia. For the Service was the central nervous system of the Stanleys themselves—it received and relayed information from the outer systems to the "brain"; helped with the formulation of official policy; and then set in motion the muscles that would deal with any particular problem. When those nerves tingled, every star, every spacelane, every planet and pocket of cosmic dust trembled and shook.

As the evidence of internal corruption mounted, it became clear that there were two courses of action. They could search patiently and painstakingly, sift through mountains of data, study the results and hope for a break—or they could plunge themselves into a trouble spot, offer themselves as bait, risk life and limb on a gamble, and trust to mind and muscle to get them out. These were the choices they had to confront . . .

But really, there was no choice—because they were d'Alemberts.

"Durward looks to be a hard nut to crack," Jules surmised as the pair were discussing strategy aboard *La Comète*. "Too many agents have been killed there already, to absolutely no gain."

"I agree," Yvette nodded. "Some rather peculiar things are going on there, and I think we might be better off if we do some background work first. We can always tackle Durward if we need to, but we'll have our feet firmly planted in facts before we do."

"Outside of Durward itself, then, I can see only three profitable points of attack: Algonia, Nevander, and Aston. Three forged Patents of Royalty, years apart. Three planets that have—coincidentally?—gained the most notorious reputations for crime and corruption."

"And," Yvette reminded him significantly, "fifty-one agents have died on those three planets alone while investigating this affair."

Jules wet his lips and spoke more quietly. "Yes, I know. Most of them were probably as smart and as skilled as we are, yet their lives went down the tubes despite all the help the local SOTE could give them . . ." He paused.

"Uh-huh. Go on. Or *because* of it."

"*Au juste*. The higher the SOTE, the tighter the security. At least in theory. But that treason in the Head's own office smelled like *l'essence de la mouffette*, if you ask me."

Yvette wrinkled her nose at just the thought of skunk perfume. "I still wish we could have taken him alive. A good stiff shot of nitrobarb would have answered a lot of interesting questions."

"So we have to find out the answers on our own. I think, for the time being, we should stay away from all SOTE contacts, except maybe for the top dog at each place. The question before the house now is, what's our best cover?"

"We'll be looked at closely, that's for sure," Yvette mused, "so we'd better pick something in keeping with our splendid physiques." She looked down at her own solidly packed form. "We can't be Earthers, not to stand inspection. Nor Delfians, more's the pity; I rather liked the cloaks and the secrecy."

"We're too obviously the products of a high-grav planet," Jules agreed. "And there haven't been too many of those settled."

"There's Purity, over in . . . where? Sector Thirty-three, I think."

Jules frowned in thought. "It's an idea, yes. That splinter group of crackpots on Purity. We can be Puritans."

"But would it work?" Yvette nibbled nervously at her lip. "They refuse to have anything to do with anybody unless there's no way to avoid it. The rest of humanity's too sinful for them. They expect everyone else, especially mother-planet DesPlaines, to be whiffed into incandescent vapor any second by the wrath of God. There *are* a lot of renegade Puritans, though—sinners who couldn't stand the 'righteous' life."

"That's what I meant. Our story will be that they kicked us out because we became too sinful. We liked to dance and play cards and drink soda pop—to say nothing of mining gold and platinum and diamonds and emeralds and bootlegging all our stuff to Earth for crass remuneration in the world of flesh. That's how we made all our money, remember?"

Yvette laughed. "Just dimly. I must have been looking the other way at the time, but you can fill me in. They *have* kicked a lot of people off Purity for doing just that—and for even smaller sins, as well. Go ahead, it's sounding better all the time."

Jules paced back and forth in the small forward cabin. "*Khorosho,* how about this? We'll get ID papers declaring us ex-Puritan Citizens of Earth—the Head can arrange that. You know how toplofty and you-be-damned Earthers are when they go out to visit 'the colonies.' "

"And we'll be toploftier and you-be-damneder than anybody," Yvette grinned wickedly. "I like it."

"Concealment by conspicuousness," her brother nodded. "But, as we know, not too many people are aware that Purity is high-grav. We'll still have to disguise our builds somewhat, particularly yours. There's lots of short, stocky men around, but you look a trifle out of place anywhere but a high-grav world."

"Then we do it the same way," Yvette said. "Obviousness. We'll flaunt ourselves at them and dare them to comment."

"Absolutely." Jules stared at himself in some imaginary mirror, trying to concoct his disguise. "Bare arms and bare legs—let them see the muscles, who cares? What do you think about hair down to my shoulders, gilded and curled

70

to a faretheewell? And a handlebar mustache, waxed to points and also gilded. Cloth-of-gold sleeveless jersey with a neckline open to the belt. Tight shorts—blue?"

Yvette shook her head. "Too common. Purple."

"Yes, purple, the color of royalty. That'll be the motif, purple and gold. Gold boots up to mid-thigh, and my entire body glistening with gold and amethyst jewelry, a million rubles' worth. People will have to close their eyes when I walk into a room."

"They do anyhow."

"Quiet, I'm still thinking. I need something to hold and wave about in the air and in people's faces. A swaggerstick, I think, a big heavy one that's got a blaster at one end and a stunner at the other. What do you think?"

Yvette considered the ensemble. "Your head's bare."

"So it is. I need a hat—a big floppy purple one with a ten centimeter wide brim and gold plumes half a meter long. And *voilà*—the complete ensemble for the well-dressed secret agent."

"I have to admit, no one would ever suspect you of being a SOTE operative in that get-up. You'd even have difficulty passing as a rational human being. I could walk right alongside you wearing a Service badge and no one would notice."

"Uh, I wouldn't recommend it . . ."

Yvette laughed. "I have no intention of it, believe me. But if you think I'm going to play little brown hen opposite that gorgeous hunk of rooster, you've soaked your cerebrum. I'll design me a costume—no, since we'll be on this for a while we'd both better have complete wardrobes —that'll knock everybody's eyes right out of their sockets. In what I'll drape my body with, no DesPlainian woman would be caught dead at a catfight."

"That's my loving sister!"

"It'll be fun. But growing your hair to shoulder length will take months, maybe a year or more. A wig?"

"Uh-uh," Jules said, shaking his head. "Too chancy. Wigs can be spotted and someone could wonder why we're doing the phony bit. I was thinking of having a growth implant done. It'll take about two months, but we've got the time. SOTE's been working on this case for sixty-seven years, and Banion— or whoever else is behind this plot— seems in absolutely no hurry to push things along. Why should he—he knows everything about us and we know

71

nothing about him. I don't think a couple of extra months will mean the difference between success and failure. And it's not as if we'll be twiddling our toes in the meantime."

"Right. We can go over the data a couple more times, plan our approach, smooth out our act—and I've got my entire wardrobe to plan. *Alors,* let's fly at it."

Thus it came about that, seven weeks later, the Executive Offices of the Duke of Algonia were invaded by a couple whose likes had never before been seen on the planet Algonia—or, for that matter, on any other planet. They arrived in style aboard the poshest spaceliner flying, the *Empress Stanley III.* Both Jules and Yvette were disappointed not to be able to use *La Comète* on this mission, but they'd agreed that public transportation would be much more in keeping with their disguise.

Jules' costume was as spectacular as he'd described and he'd developed a persona to match it. His every movement was an exaggeration; he could not seem to stand still, and even the slightest motion was embellished with wild gesticulations. His voice, when he spoke, was loud and brash, grating on the nerves of all who heard him. His tone was the epitome of supercilious snobbery. Although physically short, he was unquestionably a man who could not do things in a small way.

Yvette was, if anything, even more resplendent. She had chosen to match his color scheme of purple and gold in what little she wore, but the arrangement of the colors was the exact reverse of his. Her footwear—calf-high leather boots encrusted with amethysts and diamonds—was royal purple, sparkling and flashing as she walked. Her tight shorts—very tight and *very* short—were gold lamé. Her midriff was bare, and her breasts were supported by a shamefully thin and transparent purple silk scarf that tied behind her neck. Her belt was wide—gold backed with carlon, and heavily jeweled. A jeweled half-veil of fine gold mesh highlighted rather than hid her face. And, to cap the delectable package, her hair—which was the same rich purple as her boots and scarf—sported a tiara that would have dazzled the Empress herself, so overloaded was it with gold filigree, diamonds and amethysts. The tiara alone had been appraised conservatively at—and insured for—one million, three hundred ninety thousand rubles; yet Yvette wore it as casually as a sunbonnet.

72

Ignoring the stares of the people waiting in the long line and the sidelong glances of the office workers, the outrageous pair walked briskly up to the front desk. "We are Citizens of Earth," Jules proclaimed loudly to the startled receptionist as he courteously but firmly edged his way into the narrow space between a fat woman and the desk. The clerk was too stunned by the appearance of these apparitions to move; Jules took advantage of her indecision to lean over, pick up her hand and tuck a hundred-ruble bill neatly into it. "Carlos and Carmen Velasquez, Citizens of Earth," he repeated even more loudly, dropping two ID cards onto her desktop. "You sure do have a nice planet here, yes ma'am. 'Course, all we saw of it was on the way from the spaceport to here, but I'm a man of quick opinions. I know what I like when I see it, and I like this here Algonia, yes ma'am. Your duke wouldn't be thinking of selling it, would he?"

The poor receptionist's jaw dropped open.

" 'Course not," Jules laughed, giving her a broad wink. "Dukes don't go around selling their planets; I was just funning you. Still, this is a nice place, and my wife and me'll be happy to stay here for a while."

Yvette, who had chosen so far to stand beside her brother silently with her nose in the air, now deigned to speak. "This *is* the office where newcomers apply for sixty-day visas, is it not?"

The flustered clerk's face brightened as the conversation finally reached a level she could comprehend. "Oh no, ma'am . . . sir. That would be Gospodin Rixton's office downstairs—the SOTE, ma'am . . . sir." She seemed quite relieved to be able to shoo this duo out of her jurisdiction.

"What seems to be the trouble here?" A tall blond man with a pencil-thin mustache oozed his way across the floor to stand beside them. "Problems, Gospozha Chen?"

The girl turned to him, a "thank-you" lighting up her face. "Gospodin Rixton, these two people . . ."

"Citizens of Earth," Jules interrupted.

"They'd like to apply for a sixty-day visa."

"I'll handle it, then." He put an overly-friendly arm on Jules' shoulder and steered him out of the line. "My name is Alf Rixton, and I'm the first assistant of SOTE here on Algonia . . ."

"Delighted to meet you," Jules said loudly, pumping the man's hand. "We're Carlos and Carmen Velasquez, Citizens of Earth. We'd like to stay a couple of months on this wonderful planet of yours." He reached into his pocket and produced another hundred-ruble bill. "I trust you can arrange it for us. We'll be staying at the Hotel Splendide." He stuffed the bill very blatantly into the SOTE man's hand, then he and Yvette marched out of the room.

To their inner disgust, Rixton made no attempt to return the bribe.

CHAPTER 8

Ambush in the Park

THE STANLEY DOCTRINE. As one of her principal reforms, Empress Stanley 3 imposed on society the formal hierarchical structure still in use today. Given the fact that stratification was inevitable in any social system, she elected to introduce the arrangement that had served mankind the longest—that of hereditary nobility. Her logical mind took what was essentially a chaotic state of affairs and reorganized, simplified and, in a sense, standardized it. All inhabited space was divided into thirty-six Sectors, with Earth considered to be the center of the sphere. Each Sector is ruled by a grand duke, and may contain hundreds of planets. Single planets are ruled by dukes. Marquises rule continents or the equivalent thereof. Earls rule over what would previously have been considered states or small nations. Counts rule counties. Barons—the lowest ranking nobility—rule cities or districts. (Stanhope, Elements of Empire, *Reel 2, slot 408.)*

The Hotel Splendide was the plushest, most exclusive caravansery on Algonia. Rooms there started at two hundred rubles a night and rose sharply in price. The hotel's chef was famous throughout most of Sector Three, and it was not uncommon that meals in the Splendide's restaurant ran to seventy or eighty rubles a person. The grounds of the hotel covered more than forty hectares, and included virtually every recreational facility, licit and illicit, known to man. There was even a small private forest for guests who wanted to "commune with Nature" without going too far from civilization.

Thus it was only natural that such a hotel would become the stopping place of Carlos and Carmen Velasquez, those flamboyant and flashy Citizens of Earth. Their arrival there created a small whirlwind of activity, and they quickly established themselves as favorites of both management and staff. Not only because they settled into the penthouse suite—at a thousand rubles a night—for what promised to be a long stay; not only because they were outgoing, gregarious and fun-loving; but also because they did not seem to realize that money came in denominations smaller than fifty Imperial rubles.

Though publicly they remained unflappable, privately the scale on which they were living frightened them a bit. "We could camp half our family in here," Yvette said when first they were alone in their suite, "and still have room left over there in the corner for tumbling mats."

"It's all in a good cause, though," Jules said, going over to one of the suite's four enormous vibrobeds and sprawling out on it. "I know it's hard, but we'll have to learn to live with luxury for a while."

"I'm just afraid I'll get *used* to it, that's all!"

The two visitors quickly settled into a regular routine of seemingly relaxed activity. They never rose before eleven and, after a light brunch, engaged in games of tennis and rondola by themselves, or played in team sports with other guests. Then came a brisk swim in the indoor pool, followed by a midafternoon snack. They retired to their suite until dinner, after which they walked for at least one hour through the relatively deserted pathways of the hotel's planned forest. Unsuspicious activities for two people on a vacation for the purposes of relaxation.

But those walks in the late evening played a central role in their plans. Heretofore, all the SOTE agents who had investigated the criminal activity on Algonia had gone looking for it. They had found it, of course, but it was Yvette's theory that perhaps they had only found what was meant for them to find. Perhaps the d'Alemberts would have more success if they let the criminal activity find them.

Their hikes on the first few nights were exploratory more than anything else. But after a while they hit upon a path that they particularly liked, and stuck to it monotonously from then on. Every evening they would take their rented car and drive it from the hotel to the corner of the grounds where the forest began; then they would park it and begin their six kilometer hike along a dark, heavily-wooded area of hills and rocks. It was a route on which they encountered no other people; a route that had five places made to order for an ambush; and a route that they had gone to much trouble to publicize.

For six nights they swung along their chosen path at a steady eight-kilometers-an-hour gait, swathed in complete silence . . .

Complete silence? Yes. Their flashy but sturdy walking boots made not even a whisper of sound as they trod across the soft ground; no item of their apparel or equipment rattled or tinkled or squeaked or even rustled—everything had been designed that way. They could hear, but they could not be heard. Anyone lying in wait for them would have to spot them before moving into action—and the d'Alemberts themselves had very acute hearing and aerialists' eyesight.

As they reached a clearing with minimal potential for danger, Yvette asked, "Do you suppose we goofed, Julie?"

"Uh-uh, pretty sure not. I've learned to trust your intuitions. I think it's just taking them some time to get the operation set up. Consider: Senor and Senora Velasquez can't just disappear into thin air—it would raise entirely too many questions. Also, besides the king-sized fortunes we're wearing, everyone knows we've got enough capital tucked away in the Splendide's safe to start a bank. They'll want to get their hands on that, too. I think they'll want to use substitutes for us, after getting us out of the way—and that will take a bit of planning. We didn't specifically design these three-quarters naked outfits of ours to make it hard to impersonate us, but it worked out well that way. There aren't too many people around who could carry off that imposture."

"That's right. They'd have to check out of the Splendide, going past the entire staff that knows us well because of our tips, and pry our fortune out of the safe. Nice; I never thought of it cutting both ways. The only way they can match our physiques is to get two other DesPlainians or ex-Puritans, or people from some other heavy gravity world."

Jules nodded. "And for that, they'll have to send out. Heavy grav types like us just don't do much unessential traveling to light-grav planets. It's just not comfortable, as you and I both know. In fact, another month of this with

77

no work at grav and we'll both be as flabby as two tubs of boiled noodles."

"So let's hope it won't be a month, then. But we certainly should give them a couple more days. Anyone who thinks they can ambush us certainly deserves the opportunity to *try*."

Five more hikes proved uneventful, and the two of them began feeling very discouraged. But on the sixth evening following that conversation, at a place where the path passed close to a dense stand of trees on one side and a thick patch of underbush on the other, their straining ears heard rustling sounds and their keen eyes caught the blur of movement. "Rube!" Yvette whispered to her brother, and Jules nodded. Both were braced for action.

For concealment, the place the attackers had chosen was ideal—as the d'Alemberts had set it up to be. But in order to make their attack, the muggers would have to move—and, being of a relatively low echelon in the criminal world, they could not take effective precautions against their movements being detected. Also they had no idea whatsoever of how terribly fast their proposed quarries were.

At the first hint of activity, Yvette and Jules became lightning incarnate. Jules' hat and swaggerstick hit the ground almost instantaneously, and Yvette's tiara was right beside them. The two used their well-muscled legs as springs to catapult them in low dives, Jules to his side of the road and Yvette to hers.

Diving straight through a bush, Jules found himself in the center of a clump of five men. Four of them were in a tight configuration, with the fifth standing a short distance away. Having Jules' powerful body come flying suddenly into their midst upset them no end. As he landed, Jules slapped the nearest man on the head—but gently, so as not to break his neck. As his momentum carried him still further forward, he grabbed the shirt of this first unconscious man and pulled him along. Then, rolling quickly to his knees, he picked his victim up and hurled him bodily at another man some three meters away. The second man, hit by the ninety-five kilo mass of his compatriot, staggered backwards and fell to the ground.

Jules, of course, had not stopped to watch the effect of his throw; what was most important to him was to keep moving, to do as much damage as quickly as possible and to present as small a target as he could. Springing to his feet, he jumped straight at the third man, who cringed reflexively. Jules' powerful fist lashed out and struck his would-be assailant squarely in the solar plexus. The man *whooshed* and crumpled lifelessly to the ground. In the same motion, Jules spun, almost ballet-like, on one foot while, with the other, he kicked the fourth man in the face —not with his toe, but with the whole big flat sole of his boot. The impact crushed the man's face in and rendered him instantly unconscious.

That made the score four down and one to go. But that one would be a little more difficult, Jules realized as he peered through the darkness at his remaining adversary; this one was a DesPlainian, by the look of him—the man who had obviously been intended to substitute for "Carlos Velasquez." He had been standing several meters away from the scene of the battle, not originally intending to take part in it, and the five seconds it had taken Jules to dispose of the other crooks had given this one time to regain his senses. He had a gun drawn, but Jules couldn't tell in the darkness whether it was a stunner or a blaster.

Jules hit the ground immediately and used the darkness of the night to cover him. His opponent with the gun was moving about and making what to Jules seemed like an awful lot of noise, though the criminal hardly realized that. As a result, Jules could track his adversary by sound, and kept low. Circling around, he came up behind the man, grabbed him by the shoulder and spun him around. The man had time to register only the briefest look of surprise before Jules' right fist came smashing up under his jaw. Knowing that the man was another DesPlainian, Jules made no effort to pull his punch, and gave the hapless fellow the full strength at his command.

The DesPlainian criminal fell to the ground, his gun dropping from his hand. Jules caught the gun on the fly; it was a stunner, set on eight. A nasty setting, because it would leave a person helpless for days and could have permanent paralytic effects on the nervous system.

A movement caught his eye where there should not have been one, and Jules whirled to face the threat. The second man, at whom he'd thrown the first, was getting to his feet, gun in hand. Jules had no time to reset the controls

79

on his stunner; he fired point-blank and the man went down again. This time he lay very still.

Yvette, too, had had a busy time of it. Her dive took her between two trees and into a small crowd of people. With arms spread apart, she grabbed two heads in her hands and brought them together with a frightening crack. She rolled as she hit the ground, regained her feet and looked around. A shadow moved, and she attacked it. Bringing her knee up, she produced a sharp cry of pain from the man whose groin she had hit. As he doubled over, she grabbed him by the shoulders, lifted him over her head and flung him at a fourth shadowy figure approaching in the nighttime gloom. There was a satisfying thud as the bodies connected and collapsed on the ground.

Suddenly a blow hit her on the back of the neck. It was a hard one, as such things go, and might have inflicted serious damage on the spinal column of someone in less superb physical condition. In Yvette's case, however, those neck muscles were so tight and hard that the blow merely stunned her momentarily. She stumbled forward from the impact, but recovered her poise quickly and turned the fall into a roll. After completing her somersault, she sprang to her feet, spun around and faced her attacker.

About all she could make out in the dim starlight was the other's silhouette—but that was enough to tell her some vital facts. For one thing, the silhouette was definitely female; there was no way a male could fit into that particular assemblage of curves. For another, the short, squat form obviously belonged to a DesPlainian, or at least someone from a high-grav world. Adding these facts rapidly together in her mind, she came to the conclusion that the woman she was facing was the "ringer" brought in to impersonate her and steal her fortune. That only made sense; if the real Carlos and Carmen Velasquez were waylaid on the trail, the erstaz ones should be ready to move in instantly to take their places.

Once that conclusion was reached, however, it was pigeonholed in her mind. The main problem she faced at the moment was staying alive while incapacitating this other woman at the same time. That problem was complicated by the fact that the DesPlainian criminal most likely had a gun that she would be using any second.

Yvette dove back in the direction from which she had come, toward her attacker. As she dove, she also twisted

80

in midair, so that when she landed it was on her side, stretched out horizontally. She converted her forward momentum into a rolling motion, so that she spun along the ground directly into the legs of the woman who'd been standing there. Like a bowling ball hitting a strike, Yvette's body knocked the woman completely off her feet. The two females sprawled out on the ground in a tangle of shapely limbs.

The other girl landed on top, and tried to press an elbow into Yvette's windpipe. The SOTE agent fended off the blow with her forearm, simultaneously bringing her knee up to make a sharp blow on the other's spine. The attacking female cried out and fell over forward; Yvette clipped her on the chin as she went by, and the now unconscious ambusher tumbled loosely to the ground.

Yvette paused for a moment to regain her breath. As she got to her knees, she listened attentively for any sounds to indicate that more attackers were in the neighborhood. Only stillness reached her ears; even the normal night sounds had been hushed as the forest animals fled the scene of the fight.

Then her brother's voice came whispering its way through the darkness across the road. "Eve?" he asked tentatively. "Five here."

"Same here," she replied, springing lightly to her feet. "All smooth. Is there any clear space by you?"

"Yes—lug them over this way."

Yvette picked up two of her would-be kidnapers and hauled them to the other side of the pathway, where her brother was waiting with his victims. Jules helped carry the other three while she retrieved her tiara. In just a couple of minutes the ten unconscious or dead crooks—Jules was afraid that number eight stunner setting might have been a little too strong—were laid on their backs in a neat row.

Yvette took a miniflash out of her boot and shone it on the faces of the two people who'd meant to impersonate them. "Ugh, do we look like that? No wonder everybody stares at us. I don't think I'll ever trust a mirror again."

"They say imitation is the sincerest form of flattery," her brother pointed out.

"'They' say a lot of things that wouldn't buy you a cupful of air on market day. We'd better get down to work."

"Au juste." Jules handed her his stun-gun, on which he had turned the setting back down to three. "If you want to start working on these creeps, I'll go back and see if I can navigate the car along the path. Damn, I wish we'd been able to use our own—it would have been a lot easier to fly in here."

"But out of character," Yvette reminded him. "The Velasquezes had to rent the biggest, flashiest limousine available. Consistency above all."

Muttering something under his breath about what idiots the Velasquezes were, Jules set off along their path to where they had parked their car. Some ten minutes later the car came crawling back along the route, moving with agonizing slowness as Jules navigated its way down the narrow path trying to avoid scraping the sides on the trees and rocks. By the time he pulled up, Yvette had just finished injecting their prisoners with nitrobarb from the small kit inside her boot. "They'll be ready for questioning in twenty minutes," she said.

She helped her brother load their captives like cordwood into the back of the limousine, then guided him as he backed up the path to the highway. Once out on the open road, however, the d'Alemberts did not drive back to their hotel. Carting ten unconscious bodies through the lobby would have required a bit of explanation, even from such colorful and eccentric characters as Carlos and Carmen Velasquez.

Instead, Jules gunned their limousine on the road out of town. They had taken the opportunity soon after they arrived on Algonia to rent a country "house"—which most people would have considered a large estate—by phone from a broker. This house was so far removed from everything that they could have operated an illicit spacefield on the estate without the neighbors being any the wiser.

They unloaded their freight into the empty living room of the mansion and got down to serious business. The man Jules had shot with the number eight stunner beam was useless for their purposes, but the other nine hoodlums were just coming out of the initial coma state induced by the nitrobarb and were ready to talk. Under sharp questioning by the two expert agents—and completely unable to lie or withhold knowledge under the nitrobarb's influence—they revealed the complete details of their plan: how they had intended to waylay and kill the Velasquezes, substitute their own people for them, then have those substitutes check out of the hotel, taking all their money and jewels with them. The operation would have been perfect, had Carlos and Carmen been the people they'd seemed—but unfortunately for these crooks, the d'Alemberts were not a pair of fops.

Yvette and Jules intensified their interrogation. It took no great effort to learn the name of these people's immediate superior, a supposedly respectable stockbroker in a city over a thousand kilometers away. But they were after more information—the name of the biggest crime chief on the entire planet.

After peeling layer after layer of hierarchy, the SOTE agents got the information they were looking for, but it startled them nonetheless. The crime boss on this world was no less than the baron of the city of Osberg, which was the second largest city on Algonia.

CHAPTER 9

Storming the Castle

Along with the proliferation of titles came the elaborate system of court etiquette and rules that are the hallmark of upper classes. Rules of succession were most important. Empress Stanley 3, in an attempt to avoid as many struggles as possible, decreed that strict primogeniture be observed in all inheritances— and, being a woman herself, insisted that the primogeniture be carried out with no distinction as to sex. The heir to a title was, by courtesy, addressed by the next lowest title—the oldest child of an earl, for instance, would be a count or countess until inheriting the full title. Younger children of noble families bore the honorific titles of "Lord" or "Lady," without anything more specific, and were treated with deference. Marriage laws, too, were more relaxed than under previous oligarchical systems. Nobles could marry either commoners or nobles of higher or lower rank, and the lower-born of the pair would automatically be raised to the rank of the spouse. (Stanhope, Elements of Empire, *Reel 2, slot 409.)*

Leaving their involuntary guests trussed up and helpless in their country mansion, the d'Alemberts proceeded to drive to Osberg and, in particular, to Kräftig Castle, some two hundred and fifty kilometers away. As he drove, Jules could not help but shake his head when he thought of what they'd learned. "I knew our friends, whoever they are, wouldn't stay out of a caper with this kind of money involved. But a noble getting in on the act! Who would have thought the boss would be the Baron of Osberg?"

"You for one, brother dear," supplied Yvette. "And maybe me for another. At least we knew ·the boss traitor had to be *somebody* in a position of power. And we'd better get used to the thought of picking on the nobility; I'll bet whoever is masterminding this conspiracy has a pretty high listing in the Peerage. Banion, when we find him, will either be posing as a noble or else have the protection and patronage of one. Either way we'll have to go slow."

The Baron's castle was three kilometers outside the city of Osberg itself. Jules parked their car a good kilometer down the road and they walked in from there. Each carried a stunner taken from their ambushers and, in addition, Yvette carried her hypo kit containing enough nitrobarb to question a regiment.

They approached the stronghold cautiously, taking great care not to be seen or heard. Two phantoms in the night, they made their way to the outside of the castle walls. Kräftig Castle was an imposing edifice, four stories high and set on a steep slope. Its five hectares of ground were encircled by a reinforced concrete wall four and a half meters high that was surmounted by interlaced strands of charged barbed wire.

Jules and Yvette walked partway around the wall, sizing it up. There were two gates, front and rear, each built of five-centimeter-square bar steel and topped with more of the charged barbed wire. Neither could be opened except by electronic commands from inside the castle.

"And not even a welcome mat," Yvette whispered to her brother.

"I definitely get the impression that the good Baron doesn't care for uninvited guests. *Eh bien,* if there's no welcome mat we'll have to provide our own. Over the top?"

"Over the top," Yvette agreed.

The two grinned at each other and separated. Taking advantage of the high hedges lining the road to the back gate, they backed off some twenty meters down the path while keeping under cover. Yvette was on the left side of the roadway, Jules on the right. They could not see each other well in the darkness, but they were so used to working with one another that their reflexes worked practically in tandem. At an almost inaudible "now" from Yvette, both ran at top speed toward the wall. Two sets of legs like coiled springs bent under them as they came within two meters; then the muscles pushed off and the pair of aerialists were soaring upward into the air. Each cleared the topmost wire with a full meter to spare. They had their stunners already drawn and, at the apex of their silent flight, they sent their beams—which were set on six for a twelve-hour stun—shooting down at the guards manning the wall. Firing rapidly and precisely, they shot down every guard they saw—and the fact that the interior of the courtyard was well lit helped their aim no end.

They absorbed most of the impact of landing with their well-muscled legs, then rolled and sprang to their feet, still running. Over to their left was a smaller house, most likely the garage and servants' quarters. Yvette gave an almost infinitesimal nod of her head to indicate that she would tackle that building. Jules acknowledged her signal and ran toward the main house.

The ground floor had many windows he could have broken through, but he preferred to be a bit neater. It was the work of only a second to spot a small door that led into the pantry. The door was locked, but that didn't stop him for more than a couple of seconds more. Reaching into his pocket, he pulled out a cutting torch so small it fitted the palm of his hand. Only seven seconds were needed for its powerful laser action to burn through the lock mechanism, and the door flew open inward at his insistent push.

Jules found himself in a small storeroom for the castle's provisions. The room was refrigerated, but he had no intention of staying here. Crossing purposefully down one row of shelves, he came to another door that led outward to the kitchen. This door was unlocked, and he passed through it into the cooking area. As it was now quite late, only a small handful of servants were attending to the clean-up activities after the evening meal. These hapless folk slumped bonelessly to the floor as Jules' stunner beam hit them before they were even aware that anything untoward was happening.

Jules went through the kitchen like a purple streak, then rode an elevator tube up to the next level. He passed through the dining room without encountering anyone else and raced down a small service hallway until he came to a set of thick velvet curtains. Putting his eye to the crack between the curtains, he observed the activity in the next room.

The main hall of the castle was immense. Its beamed

ceiling and paneled walls were of waxed yellow-wood; the light from the hundreds of electric false candles in the three wrought-iron chandeliers glinted off those walls and made the whole room bright and sparkling. The floor was of polished brown marble in swirling, indefinable patterns. Long divans upholstered in plush tawny velvets graced the floor at appropriate intervals. At the far end of the room was a fireplace that looked big enough to sleep two people in comfort; at the moment, however, a two-meter log was burning there, doing its best to warm the chill of the room. The walls were tastefully adorned with modernistic paintings, and above the mantlepiece was the antlered head of some animal Jules didn't recognize.

Eleven men were in that hall, some sitting, some standing. The air was hazy from the smoke of the different types of cigarets they were puffing, and partially empty glasses attested to the amounts of alcohol being consumed. The men talked only occasionally, and then mostly in monosyllables; they checked their watches frequently, and definitely appeared to be waiting for someone or something.

If they're expecting news about the Velasquez kidnaping, thought Jules, *they'll get it in a very startling way.* Bringing up his stunner and taking careful aim, he shot them all in quick succession. Eleven bodies collapsed limply into their chairs or onto the floor.

Jules went quickly back to the pantry door to rendezvous with his sister. "Everything's *khorosho* outside," she reported. "I caught most of them in bed. Now for the big frisk."

Moving rapidly, but without sloppy hastiness, the pair of agents searched the entire castle from subcellar to garrets. They moved with stunners drawn and ready, and when they had gone through an area they *knew*, beyond doubt, that everyone in it was unconscious. Within an hour, everyone —guards, servants, guests and family—everyone within the outer wall except for themselves was out cold. Then and only then did Jules walk over to the communicator on the wall of the main hall, cut off its video circuit, and punch out a special number.

"This is the Service of the Empire," a perfectly trained, beautifully modulated female voice came from the speaker. "Would you please turn your vision on and let me know how I may serve you?"

Instead of complying with the request for visual, Jules

said succinctly, "Sote six. Affold abacus zymase bezant. The head depends upon the stomach for survival."

"Bub-bub-but sir . . ." The change in the girl's voice was shocking. She had never heard—and had never thought she would hear—those four six-letter code words spoken together; and coupled with the words "head" and "survival" they tended to daze her for a moment. She rallied quickly, though. "He's home asleep, sir, but I'll get him right away. One moment, please," and Jules heard the insistent beeping of a personal pager signalling its master.

"Lemme 'lone," a sleepy voice protested. "G'way. Cut out the damn beeping or . . ."

"Gospodin Borton! Wake up!" the girl almost screamed. *"Please* wake up! It's a Sote six," and she repeated the four code words.

"Oh." That had done it. *"Khorosho,* Phyllis; thanks."

"You are connected, sirs," the girl informed them, "and I'm not. Signal green, please, when you are through." Jules smiled tightly. He could tell from her voice that she'd take a beating rather than eavesdrop on the conversation that was to follow, even if she had been able to understand it.

"Praxis," Borton said, requesting identification, symbol or some sign of their authority.

"Wombat and Periwinkle." (Their own identifying symbols.)

"Holy . . ." Borton began, but shut himself up. Those code names were almost legendary, and he had never thought he'd ever meet them. They were the very top skimmings of the smoothest cream of the entire Service! *"Khorosho."*

"Rafter, angles, angels. Angled. Suffer. Harlot static invert, cosine design. Single-joyful, singer, status, stasis. Over."

There was dead silence at the other end of the line for three seconds; then they heard Borton gulp and say, "Excuse me for not answering quicker. All of that takes a little time to sink in. It's fantastic, but you didn't say where you are."

"We didn't know your local grid coordinates, and proper names don't encode too easily. Let me think. Kinder rafter argent faster talent indent ghosts. Carbon assign silver tender leader exempt. Got that?"

"Quite. That's good improvisation."

88

"Come through the front gate. Do a code O on your lights so we'll know it's you. Over and out if it's *khorosho*."

"Perfectly *khorosho*," Borton said—and it was. If Agents Wombat and Periwinkle told any planetary chief of SOTE to go jump in the lake he'd do it—and fast. "Here's your green, Phyllis. Thanks."

It took Borton forty-five minutes to get dressed, assemble a squad of men, and get over to the castle. The d'Alemberts used that intervening time to good advantage. Even while Jules had been talking, Yvette had been quietly going about her business, injecting each of their eleven top prisoners with doses of nitrobarb. After twenty minutes, they were ready to tell everything they knew. Unfortunately, except for the Baron, all of them knew very little. This criminal organization has been built on a cell system, with people in one group not knowing anyone from any of the others except for the one person directly above them in the hierarchy.

Even the Baron himself, the man in charge of this whole planet's underworld, only knew of one off-world contact, but that was better than nothing. Under the drug's influence, the Baron told them about a certain bar near the main spaceport on the planet Aston, and about the code phrase necessary to get beyond a certain point.

Finally Borton's party showed up at the front gate. The planetary chief blinked the headlights on his vehicle three short blinks, as agreed, and the gates opened for him. He and his men entered the estate and walked quickly to the front door of the castle.

Jules and Yvette allowed only him to see them as they admitted him to the vestibule; the rest of his men were told to wait outside. Borton recognized them instantly. "You!" he exclaimed, looking from one spectacular agent to the other and back again. "You two have been driving my office staff nuts trying to get a line on you. I must admit, it is a switch. You came in with bands blaring and pennons waving."

"Absolutely. We figured they'd be looking for people who skulked around in dark corners."

"Could be . . . If I may ask, I suppose there's a good reason why I wasn't let in on any of this from the beginning?"

"Very good. Follow us and you'll see what it was," Jules said.

They led Borton into the main hall. The eleven bodies lay scattered about the floor in a drugged stupor. Borton took just a quick skim to size up the situation, then turned back to the d'Alemberts. "You used nitrobarb," he said. His tone was matter-of-fact, though many people could not mention the drug's name without either distaste or horror. "And on the Baron of Osberg, yet. With nitrobarb's fatality rate, half of them will die. I think I can see now why you didn't apply for approval first."

"They'll *all* die," Jules said grimly. "Especially the Baron. The penalty for treason, remember, is summary execution. Those who survive the drug may live a few days longer than the others. That's all. But you don't really see yet. Keep on looking."

Borton gazed back into the hall. As his eyes swept over the slack jaws and glazed expressions of the drugged men, they eventually came to rest on the tall, burly figure of a blond man with a pencil-thin mustache. There they stopped, and Borton's face turned gray. The shock and surprise hit him so hard that he couldn't even think to swear.

"That's Alf Rixton," he managed finally. "My first assistant. He's been with me for over ten years! Top clearance, too, with lie detector and hypnointerrogation every year. He's done splendid work."

"Yeah—for the other side," Yvette said coldly. "The only crooks and traitors he ever caught were the ones his people wanted to get rid of. It's all yours now, Borton, the whole operation. Take over. We'll have to stay on-planet for a while—some people higher up might get a bit suspicious if the Velasquezes left Algonia the instant this ring was broken—but we don't want to appear in this. Not so much as a whisper. Nobody here in the castle got a look at us—we moved a little too fast for them—and your men haven't seen us. Only you know, and you won't tell. But there are a few others you'll have to silence for a time, if not permanently." She told him about the ambushers who were now trussed up on the Velasquezes' hideaway estate.

Borton nodded. "Don't worry, they'll be taken care of. But listen, how can I explain all of this? There'll be reports to fill out and the press will be asking all sorts of questions. They get very sharp whenever the nobility's involved in scandal. What can I say? They won't believe I planned this whole operation by myself."

"Of course not," Jules grinned. "Gospodin Rixton over

there cooked the whole thing up and helped you pull it off. A fury with a short fuse as he waded into the thick of the fighting. Too bad the honors are posthumous, but he died upholding the glorious traditions of the Service."

Again, Borton nodded—more slowly, this time. "Thanks. One of our very best men, he died a hero's death, defending gallantly and so forth—sob, sob—the rat. Yeah, that'll do it. But having me take the credit for this operation when the two of you really did all the work . . ."

"It really wouldn't be wise to let people know we'd been here," Yvette said quietly.

"*Khorosho,*" Borton grinned wryly. "Undercover agents should remain under cover."

"Exactly," Jules agreed. Then he looked at his sister and, in unison, they recited the Service salute: "Here's to tomorrow, fellow and friend. May we all live to see it!" And with that, they strode out of the room, out of the castle without being seen by Borton's men—and out of Borton's life forever. One scum pit had been cleaned out— it was time for them to move onward and upward to the next.

Borton stood motionless, staring at the door as it closed behind them. He knew *what* those two were—Agents Wombat and Periwinkle—but that was all he knew, or ever would know, about them. But they had given him too much to do to waste his time woolgathering. He had to interrogate these prisoners, find out more about their organization so that he could sweep up the pawns as well as the kings, and concoct a story that would satisfy the press.

He let the rest of his men into the house and barked his orders. Then, shrugging his shoulders, he began questioning those of the hoodlums who were still alive.

News of the arrests broke early the next morning. Involving as it did the treason of a rich and important baron, all the news services leapt at it. Words flashed through the subether at many times the speed of light, and soon the information was being broadcast as a major scandal on every fully settled planet of the Empire.

In particular, the news reached a tall, angular man to whom it was more than just a piece of sensationalism. He lost no time in taking his private elevator tube to the subbasement, where his private map of the Empire glowed. He stood there looking up at its enormous bulk, his dark eyes scanning the pinpoints of light that represented planets. At first he couldn't find the green dot that represented Algonia, one of his key systems—then he understood. His computers had already assimilated the data coming in from all parts of his domain, and had reassessed the situation. The dot that was Algonia no longer burned the green of one of his key planets, nor even the red that indicated he controlled it. That dot was a clear, steady blue—the blue that represented the Empire.

A setback, the man thought as he stroked his goatee. *A definite setback. But hardly a crucial one.* He felt comforted as he looked upward at his three-dimensional map. There were still more than two dozen green lights, still close to a thousand red ones. His crimson tide was still growing in magnitude, still threatening to engulf the few remaining spots of blue. The loss of one green light could hardly stop his inexorable progress.

The question remained, though, burning in the back of his brain: was the loss of Algonia a coincidence, or did it form a part of some counteroffensive against him? It would be hard to tell from this isolated incident; he would have to set his computers to look for a pattern.

For some unexplained reason, the late Colonel Grandon crossed his mind. The traitor had said something about a special team of two agents. Could they in some way have been responsible for this affair? It was something to correlate, surely.

But he was not worried. Even if, somehow, two agents acting on their own could wipe out an entire planetary organization, they still could not begin to touch the entire structure of what he had built. *Besides,* he gloated, *there are plenty of boobytraps along the way.*

CHAPTER 10

The Switch

*One of the most controversial provisions of the
Stanley Doctrine was the one regarding marriages.
Nobles were free to marry anyone they chose, whether
the chosen was noble or common. Royalty did not
have this freedom. (In fact, this is the only limitation
placed on royalty in the entire document.) Members
of the royal family were required to marry commoners. Moreover, the Stanley family name was to be
retained even when a princess married; in that one case
alone, the male changed his surname. This provision
was considered shocking when it was announced, but
the reasoning behind it was sound. Empress Stanley 3
wanted to avoid the inbreeding that had absolutely
destroyed the European monarchies by the twentieth
century C.E. By absolutely forbidding marriage within
a consanguinity of one thirty-second, she insured the
continuing strength of the Stanley line. (Stanhope,*
Elements of Empire, *Reel 2, slot 411.)*

No one at the Hotel Splendide saw the Velasquezes return
to the hotel that night, but that was not unusual; they had
sometimes in the past come in via the garage and gone
straight up to their suite on a private elevator tube. Nor did
anything seem unusual when they came down to breakfast
at their usual time of eleven o'clock the next morning.
There was a difference, though, in that they had actually
slept that late this morning—they'd earned it.

Of course, Carmen and Carlos knew nothing of the
arrests of the night before when the eager waiter hurried
into the dining room with the breakfast they had punch-
ordered ahead from their room. They could tell that something important had happened by the fact that he was

accompanied this time by his captain, who carried both local morning newsrolls in his hand.

"Good morning, gospodin and gospozha," the captain said respectfully. "You have perhaps not yet heard the extraordinary news on your receiver?"

"Uh-uh." Jules covered a yawn with his hand and shook his head. "We're hardly awake yet." He was dressed in gold satin pantaloons and a short purple vest; Yvette wore her fabulous headpiece and a purple-and-gold morning robe that, while opaque in a few places here and there, was practically transparent everywhere else.

"Did something happen that concerns us?" Yvette asked languidly.

"Most assuredly. It is something that rocks the faith of every honest citizen. The most tremendous, the most sensational scandal the Empire has seen in twenty years—and it happened right here on Algonia!" He put the newsrolls down beside Yvette while he helped the waiter arrange the breakfast table most meticulously. "But perhaps I intrude. You will read of it later, I'm sure. You will naturally now want to eat your breakfast while it is still hot. Forgive me for intruding." The two hotel men accepted the Velasquezes' usual generous gratuities and left the pair in peace.

After their meal, Jules and Yvette went back up to their suite and read through the story with great interest—and also with an occasional snort or giggle. The official version was, of course, new to them, but they had to admit that Borton had done a credible job in fabricating it. SOTE, under the masterly direction and leadership of its planetary chief, had been keeping this band of traitors under close and continuous surveillance for over a year. They had waited until they were sure they had found every member and connection of the band, and then had struck at every point simultaneously. They had made a clean sweep.

Faced with the absolute proof of their guilt, each of the traitors had confessed fully. The Service, acting in its capacity as administrator of the Emperor's justice, promptly carried out the mandatory sentence for treason: death. That sentence even included the Baron of Osberg, who had been the group's ringleader. Normally he would have been entitled, as a peer of the realm, to a High Court of Justice; but so overwhelming was the evidence against him that he

94

broke down, confessed his crimes and was permitted to take the "honorable" way out.

The news report hastened to point out that the Baron was the only member of his family to be involved in these treasonous activities, and so his barony would not revert to the Crown. Instead, his wife became the Baroness Dowager Carlotta, and his daughter Ilse—only nineteen year old—became the new Baroness. Ilse was known as a kind, generous woman, active in sports as well as in numerous philanthropic organizations, and would give Osberg the new, dynamic leadership it needed—and so on.

Planetary Chief Borton had had only the help of his brave assistant, Alf Rixton; none had come from Earth. No suggestion was made anywhere that nitrobarb had been used—and for good reason. The mere possession of that powerful drug had been made a capital offense some fifteen years earlier.

"Nice," Yvette said. "That story's so tight I almost believe it myself."

"Yeah," sighed Jules, leaning back on his bed. "But now comes the roughest part of all—waiting. I'd love nothing better than to move on to Aston and follow up that lead we got from the Baron . . . it could dry up before we can move. But we're stuck here for a while at least because we can't draw attention to ourselves. If Carlos and Carmen left right after this raid, somebody might put two and two together to get twenty-two."

Yvette thought for a moment. "I know that's what I told Borton last night, but I'm not so sure right now. The fact that we were here on Algonia—coupled with the fact that those two 'Delfians' in the Dunedin Arms could only have been a high-grav twosome—would be plenty of evidence already for people not half as smart as the ones we're up against. It won't take the enemy too long to associate the Velasquezes with the Delfians. So whether we stay here a month or leave today makes no difference—except, perhaps, as an exercise in the old guessing game."

"Tu as raison, as always. But, as you said, the old guessing game can be important, and I think we should take some time to set up some sleight of hand. Let's put in a call back home and see what we can arrange, shall we?"

It was eight days later that Carlos and Carmen Velasquez bid a tearful farewell to the Hotel Splendide. Tears were plentiful on the other side of the counter as well, because the staff knew they might never again encounter such heavy tippers. True to their fashion, the dizzy pair of ex-Puritans scattered their parting largesse from the penthouse all the way to their limousine, and thence to the spaceport.

Once there, they boarded a luxury liner bound for Lateesta via Aston. As the ship's last port of call had been DesPlaines—and as it had taken on some passengers there —sections of the vessel had been marked out for artificial gravity. Feeling what they considered to be the only honest gravitational pull after so long made Jules and Yvette considerably homesick; but that homesickness was at least in part alleviated in a couple of minutes when they visited the suite of the three passengers who had traveled here from DesPlaines.

The door to the suite opened, and there stood a small, powerfully-built girl with brown hair, almond-shaped eyes and an exquisitely beautiful face. That face lit up with surprise and delight as the girl belatedly recognized the pair standing before her.

"Jules!" she shrieked, and leaped at him so suddenly that even with his strength he had to take a step back to maintain his balance.

"Vonnie! Sweetheart!" His arms clasped around her solid—but decidedly feminine—body as their lips met in a passionate kiss. Time froze for them for maybe half a minute as the two young people renewed their love after a four-month separation.

After being motionless in each other's arms for so long, Yvonne Roumenier pulled back a little, looked Jules up and down with critical eyes, and finally shook her head. "I have *got* to have a picture of you like that. Both of you," she added, seeming to notice Yvette for the first time. The two girls kissed affectionately on the cheek. "Come on in," Yvonne said, opening the door wider to admit them.

The stateroom was first-class, but not the deluxe one that the "Velasquezes" had taken, several levels away. The furniture was all comfortably upholstered and solidly built; it had to be to withstand the three gees of artificial gravity within the room.

"They told me you'd disguised yourselves," Yvonne continued, "but *this* is something that has to be seen to be believed. Gabby, Jacques, come on out here and see the pair of peacocks who dropped by."

As the two people so addressed entered the room, Yvonne continued to look at Jules. "You always were a handsome so-and-so, Julie, but now you're simply *beautiful!*" She kissed him a few more times. "But I'm not wild about that mustache—it tickles."

"You'll get used to it," Jules smiled back at his fiancée. "I did."

The two other people who now entered the room were both DesPlainians, with the short, stocky bodies that characterized inhabitants of that planet. The woman was Gabrielle d'Alembert, sister-in-law to Jules and Yvette. Her husband was their older brother Robert, heir to the Duke's title and the man who really ran DesPlaines while the Duke was off managing the Circus. Gabrielle had an aristocratic tilt to her nose and steel-gray eyes that could be quite cold, though they seemed friendly enough right at the moment. She was slightly older than Yvette, though she kept her skin so smooth and perfect that they might have been sisters in fact as well as in law.

The man beside her was Jacques Roumenier, Yvonne's younger brother. Both the Roumeniers were children of one of Duke Etienne's best friends, Baron Ebert Roumenier of Nouveau Calais; they themselves were lifelong friends of Jules and Yvette and had, in fact, been raised together. They were also cracking good SOTE agents.

Jacques was a slightly horsefaced man, homely but nice. His face now sported the same type of mustache as Jules'. "Hello, Yvette," he said softly, gazing intently at her feet. Jacques had always had a crush on her and, while she loved him as a friend, her feelings did not extend beyond that—and he knew it. She was always warm and compassionate with him, though, for she hated to hurt him any more than necessary.

"Hello, Jacques," she beamed back at him. "You know, there's something about that mustache that looks familiar."

"Of course," said Yvonne, leaping into the conversational breach. "He's going to be the new Carlos, and Gabby's going to replace you. I asked the Duke to let me be Carmen Velasquez—begged him, practically on my knees—but the dirty mudlug wouldn't listen. He went by the thousand point test, like always, and Gabby's nine ninety-three beat me out."

Jules grinned. "Did you think he'd skip the scores on something this important?"

"Well, he certainly *ought* to've given me the job, since I've got nine eighty-nine and I'm engaged to his son, the only thousand-pointer alive."

"I'm still proud of you, darling," he cooed, slipping his arms around her delicate waist. "You're still more than enough woman for me to handle."

Then he looked up and smiled at the two newcomers. "Hi, Gabby; hi, Jacques," he said, giving them the belated salutation.

" 'Gabby' indeed," said Gabrielle, pulling herself up to her full aristocratic height of one hundred and sixty-four centimeters. "That's Marchioness Gabrielle to you, varlet. I don't think I'll deign to speak to any of the common herd any more unless they come crawling, bumping their foreheads on the floor." Her words were haughty, as was her tone, but there was a slight sparkle to her eyes that indicated she was joking.

"Hear, hear," Yvonne said, to which Yvette added, "That's telling him, Gabby." Then in a slightly more wistful vein, she went on, "You know, I *liked* wearing these jewels and that tiara and stuff, damn it. They did something for me."

"Yeah," Jules commented. "They blinded everyone in the room so that they wouldn't have to look at you. By the way, where's the rest of the group we ordered?"

"There wasn't any point to sending them along on a posh ship like this; Rick said that he and his boys would meet you directly on Aston," Vonnie said.

Jules and Yvette briefed Jacques and Gabrielle on the personal habits and idiosyncrasies of Carlos and Carmen, and what would be expected of them. "Can't you tell us what this whole affair is about?" Gabrielle asked.

"Sorry, can't even leak it to family. You'll find out when it's all over, I suppose. In the meantime, I'm afraid you'll just have to settle for being decoys."

Jules and Yvette escorted their replacements secretly back to their cabin, where they turned over the Velasquez wardrobe and lifestyle to the new people. They had their hair dyed back close to the original brown coloring and had it restyled so that it would be long and straight. Jules had his mustache trimmed as well; it looked much better after it had been unwaxed and uncurled, and Yvonne commented favorably on it. By the time they donned their shapeless brown homespun trousers and jackets, there was not a trace of Carlos or Carmen left in them. They looked, instead, like somewhat unorthodox but still practicing Puritans.

Any enemy spies at the landing field on Aston would have noted nothing suspicious. The Velasquez couple stayed in their cabin the whole time, their ultimate destination being Lateesta. A man and a woman from some heavy gravity planet did disembark, but they could hardly be the same two.

Meanwhile, the new Carlos and Carmen Velasquez traveled on to Lateesta, halfway across the Empire, where they continued their practice of tossing fifty-ruble bills around like confetti—and where they did nothing else suspicious whatsoever.

Jules and Yvette took adjoining rooms at a small local hotel, and awaited the arrival of their cousin, Richard d'Alembert, and his team of circus wrestlers. Word had come that they would arrive on a ship tomorrow; in the meantime, Jules and Yvette made not a single move in the direction of the bar that was their next target.

Jules had cleared the few movable items of furniture in his tiny room out of the way so that he had a path to pace. He always thought better, he claimed, when he was moving. His fists were jammed deep within his pockets and his eyes were focused intently on the floor as he strode back and forth over the cheap carpeting. Yvette sat on the edge of his single bed, her brow knit and her lips in a frown of concentration. Their new quarters were something of a letdown after their previous accommodations, but neither really noticed.

"I just can't help feeling that it's like fighting fog," Jules said aloud. "We knocked out an entire planetary organization after a couple of weeks' work, and what did we get for it? The contact point for the head of the organization on one other planet. Period. There's close to fourteen hundred planets in the Empire. If we continue on at the same rate, we'll have the whole mess cleared up in only fifty-six years—after which we'll probably have to start the job all over again, because we can't expect Banion to be standing still while we mow down his organization. He'll rebuild as fast as we knock down."

"He's getting along in years, you know. He could die first."

"In that case, he'd make his move against the Throne before his death—and if we just keep nibbling around the edges, we won't do him any damage at all. There's got to be some other way to go about this."

Yvette looked up at him speculatively. "You know, I had a dream last night about Uncle Marcel."

Just stopped pacing and looked quizzically at her. What could the Circus' magician have to do with their problem?

"You know the key part of his act, the word he's always harping on?"

"I should; I was always hanging around his tent as a kid," Jules smiled. He let his voice take on a high-pitched, nasal twang in imitation of his uncle. " 'Misdirection is the key. I tell you to watch one hand and something pops out in the other.' Yes, I think I see what you're getting at."

He scowled and resumed his pacing. "It *is* very pat. In sixty-seven years of investigation—and pretty intensive investigation, at that—every single scrap of evidence points at the planet Durward as the source of all the problems. Whenever a top agent would go to Durward and get close to anything, he would disappear without a trace. Indicating, presumably, that there is something on Durward being guarded so heavily and so well that none of our people can get near it."

"Like perhaps the Patent."

"But would it be there at all? Let's look at a couple of other things. Aimée Amorat disappeared with her son Banion after their abortive coup against her husband, Duke Henry of Durward. Over the next sixty-seven years, an Empire-wide criminal organization builds up . . ."

"And that sort of thing takes cash!" Yvette interrupted excitedly. "Even assuming that the Beast stashed away a lot of loot she embezzled from her husband—and as I recall there were some missing funds—she would have needed hundreds of billions . . . no, *trillions* of rubles to build it up as big as it is now."

"Of course, much of it could have been expected to pyramid along the way."

"Even so, she and her son would have needed help. Either they had someone from the start—and with her connections at court that wouldn't be altogether unlikely— or else they latched onto someone very quickly."

"And someone high up," Jules said pensively. "They would need a power base to work from, too. They would need someone with the authority to conceal facts and misdirect snoopers, someone who already had an organization spread out over wide volumes of space, someone who could act with relative impunity and move about freely."

"We are talking," Yvette enunciated clearly, "about a grand duke."

"That's the way I added it up, too." He stopped pacing again and leaned against a bureau, facing his sister. "Only a grand duke would have the widespread organization that could serve as a basis for what Banion has built up. Only a grand duke would have the initial resources to build this up so big in one lifetime."

"If this is true, then, the work will get a lot harder than it's been. After all, we can't go sticking nitrobarb into grand dukes at random. There's only thirty-six of them, and they're bound to be missed."

"True, but there may be another approach. If it really is Banion behind all these machinations—and all the evidence points that way—then he must be preparing for a takeover of the Empire. He's getting old, and he will want his share of glory before he goes. No matter how impressive that Patent is, he'll need a lot more than that behind him before he could succeed. He'll need manpower, he'll need arms and he'll need ships."

"Those can all be disguised as other things. He could hide whole armies as maintenance men inside factories, guns could be buried until needed, battleships could be listed as freighters . . ."

Jules nodded. "But," he said significantly, "there is something you can't hide from an expert: cash flow. If there is a coup in the works, it will show up in finances in various ways—a little too much money being spent here, one area becoming unexplainably richer than another, a stockpiling of funds over there . . ."

"We'll hit them with accountants!" Yvette exclaimed.

"Why not? It's a time-honored method."

"Little brother, you are a genius."

"It's still only the wildest of guesswork, so far," Jules hedged. "We don't *know* any of this."

"It's feeling righter and righter to me every second. SOTE has been barking up the wrong tree for more than half a century, and all forty-seven of those reels of data are junk. I think we ought to send out the word to the Head tonight and tell him to get cracking."

"We'd better have a system worked out first. Let's see, Durward is in Sector Ten, Algonia is in Three, Aston's in Six, Nevander's in Thirteen, and Gastonia is a rim-world clear to hellangone out on the edge of Twenty."

Yvette looked at him, startled. "Hold on a second. Durward, Algonia, Aston and Nevander have all appeared in this investigation before somewhere, but you left me two jumps behind you with Gastonia. Where did that come from?"

"My own twisted mind. Empress Stanley Five started exiling rebels there way back in the late twenty-two hundreds, and that practice has been followed more or less faithfully ever since. A century and a half of rebel mentality is ample breeding ground for treason. What could be a better place for Banion to recruit from?"

"*Khorosho,* then here's what we'll do. We message the Head tonight to check out the growth curves and financial statements of every planet and sector for the last seventy years. That'll take manpower, I know, but he's got it and this case has priority. His computers will work overtime. Then he takes the top six or seven and hands them over to his best financial analysts for detailed scrutiny."

"And in the meantime," Jules picked up her scheme, "we'll continue on with what we were originally intending tomorrow, until we find out what the Head has learned from these little audits. Then we'll revise our plans accordingly."

"What if we learn more facts tomorrow that point directly to Durward?"

"Then," Jules said slowly, "I'd take it as a sign that we were *meant* to go to Durward, and that the planet is really a trap for us. So we'll go anywhere *but* there."

There was one thought that neither voiced, yet both were thinking. If this new theory was right, and some grand duke or duchess were behind the whole affair, then the trail would lead inevitably right back to Mother Earth itself.

CHAPTER 11

The Blinding Flash and the
Deafening Report

All explored space was divided into thirty-six wedge-shaped sectors, the line common to all sectors being the line through the center of Sol perpendicular to the plane of the Earth's orbit. Each sector was owned, subject only to the whims of the Throne, by a grand duke. The planets of Sol's system—and particularly Earth, the most important planet of the Empire—were the private property of the Throne. Each grand duke had a palace, several residences and a Hall of State on Earth. Since most administration was done on the mother planet, it was not uncommon that the grand dukes seldom left it and traveled but rarely into the sectors of space that were their dominions. If the system encouraged absenteeism, it also kept incompetents happily away from doing any real harm. (Singh, The Historical Basis of Feudalism, *Reel 2, slot 48.)*

Midafternoon of the next day they received a call from their cousin Richard. He and five other men of his wrestling troupe had just gotten in and were awaiting further instructions. Jules told them what their target was to be, but that it wouldn't be opened until late in the afternoon. Richard grinned at him from the videoscreen of the communicator hook-up and said that he and his boys would spend the interim preparing for trouble.

The hours dragged by for the impatient d'Alemberts, but eventually the time came to act. Jules was dressed inconspicuously in a beige shirt and brown knee britches, while Yvette settled for a loose, canary yellow blouse and green and yellow plaid slacks. Neither was dressing to be showy, this time; their only concern was how well they would be able to move in what they were wearing. They strapped blasters on in concealed holsters, wanting to be prepared for anything; and, thus attired, they left their hotel for their destination.

The Cobweb Corner was a bar down in the spaceport section of Rollon, Aston's capital city. It represented a transition point in taste between the brusque vulgarity of the docks and the more delicate sensitivities of the middle class. As a result, it really pleased no one, though it had a regular clientele. The neighborhood was an uncertain one, not knowing whether to appear tough or respectable.

Having just opened for the day, the bar was still nearly empty. A couple of junior grade officers from the new ships in port had stopped by for a quick drink before going on about any other business in town, and one of them had struck up a casual conversation with a *dyevka*, one of the handful of girls who plied their own trade here. Six bouncers sat in various places around the room, keeping a seemingly casual eye on what took place here; but it was an unusual coincidence that all six of them were Des-Plainians. Since that planet is known for the strength and agility of its citizens, a more than casual observer would wonder what was so special here that needed such special guarding.

Rick and his men entered, looking for all the world like spaceship crewmen on leave. Though they were obviously also DesPlainians, no one thought it unusual that they were here. DesPlainians might be allergic to alcohol, but there were plenty of other legal substances available to cloud and relax their minds, and DesPlainians were as fond of bars as most other people.

Rick's team came in and quickly spread out over the room. A couple of them talked to the girls, who were interested in the possibility of grabbing an early customer before the real rush started. A few others ordered non-alcoholic stimulants and sat at scattered tables, nursing their drinks.

A few minutes later, Jules and Yvette entered, looking just like any ordinary middle-class couple stopping by for a quick drink before going on to a restaurant or play. How could the guards have suspected anything? Or the brains of the outfit, either, since the d'Alemberts had pitched them such a nice curve? There was no evidence that the Velasquez pair had had anything to do with what had happened on Algonia; and even if they had, they were nowhere near here—their ship had already left for Lateesta, a totally unimportant planet as far as the mob was concerned.

As they walked in, Yvette muttered something in Jules' ear and started toward the back of the bar where the powder rooms were. Jules, meanwhile, strolled casually up to the bar. There was only one bartender on duty at this hour, and he came over to inquire as to Jules' preferences. "I was told," Jules said in a quiet but distinct voice, "to ask for the Blinding Flash and say that the Deafening Report sent me."

Within a split second, the room exploded into action. Those words, coming from the lips of a man who had no business to be saying them—or even knowing them— meant a breach of security, something which had to be corrected instantly. The six bouncers sprang to life; but the d'Alembert wrestlers were faster yet. Before any of the guards could get his blaster even halfway into action he was struck by more than a hundred and fifty kilograms of the hardest-muscled body he'd ever felt.

At the same instant, the barkeep reached under the counter to grab for his own blaster—but, not being a DesPlainian himself, his reactions were abysmally slow. Jules had vaulted over the bar and wrestled the man quickly to the ground. He crooked his elbow around the bartender's neck and held it in a vise-like grip. That unfortunate gagged weakly, but Jules made sure he could take in enough air to keep him conscious. By this time, too, he had drawn his own blaster and was waving it ominously in the direction of the bystanders—the girls and the ship's officers who were bewildered by this sudden violent turn of events. They responded to Jules' gesture with immediate obedience and pacifism, so he did not worry too much about them.

Yvette, too, had not been idle during the fracas. Her supposed jaunt to the powder room had been a ruse to bring her near the door to the downstairs office when the action started. The moment she heard Jules utter the code phrase, she acted. Without even waiting to see how her brother was doing, she slammed her powerfully packed body against the office door. It splintered and broke under her assault, sending her flying into the tiny cubicle where,

105

as their informant had told them, a man sat lazily at a PBX board. He heard, more than saw, her entrance and jerked upright, reaching for a special switch at the top of his panel, but his motion was far too late—Yvette had drawn her blaster and one squeeze of the trigger had left him with just a pile of unrecognizably burned flesh sitting atop his neck.

The man had not even been wearing the headset—a very lax security agent. Yvette picked the earphones off the board and put them on her head. Then she pushed the dead body off the chair and sat down at the board to await further developments.

Back in the bar, the battle raged. It was a short one, but furiously fought. The place was a shambles in less than thirty seconds, as the combatants bowled their way through the furniture and fixtures. When a mass of three hundred kilograms—representing the combined weights of two embattled DesPlainian free-style brawlers—strikes some rather ordinary furniture, it is the furniture that breaks, not the men. In the entire room, only two tables and a half a dozen chairs remained intact; one savagely warring pair had gone straight through the heavy yellow-wood bar itself.

Jules stood behind the bar, watching the scene with amusement. He still had his left arm around the bartender's neck while holding his blaster loosely in his right hand as he watched the carnage taking place before him. His keen eyes studied the battle with careful appreciation, for he had not the slightest doubt about the outcome. Those guards were good, tough DesPlainians, but they were not d'Alembert—and those six d'Alemberts were the pick of the hardest-trained troupe of no-holds-barred fighting wrestlers known to man. Only one result was possible.

After three and a half minutes, The Cobweb Corner was fit only for a lumber yard. Tables and chairs were splintered and strewn about the floor, and the glass from broken bottles crunched underfoot. Small pools of liquid made the footing hazardous at best. But the battle was over, with the six bouncers lying unconscious on the floor. The winners of the contest sported a few eyes that would soon be black, some contusions and abrasions, and miscellaneous cuts, tears, scratches, gouges and bites that were bleeding more or less freely—but they had sustained no major injuries at all.

"Nice work, fellows. Thanks," Jules said as the last of

the wrestlers got to his feet, grinning broadly. These strapping men loved a good fight. "Treat yourself to something on the house, if you can find anything left. I think there may be a few ginger ale bottles left around unbroken." Noticing the bar's patrons still huddled, frightened, in one corner, he added, "Our apologies for the disturbance, folks. You know how these little squabbles can get out of hand. Rick, see what you can do about rounding up some champagne for these good people. On the house, of course."

Then, lifting the petrified bartender by the shirt front with one hand, he went on quietly, "As for you, comrade, I think we have a little talking to do in private. Come with me." That poor wight actually had little choice in the matter, as Jules carried him bodily into the back room where Yvette awaited them.

The d'Alemberts waited for a second as the barkeep stared goggle-eyed at the remains of the PBX operator on the floor. When they were certain the lesson had sunk in, Jules placed both his huge hands with uncomfortable tightness around the man's throat. "Now then, I'd like a little information—namely, what sort of protective gizmos are there between this room and the boss's office upstairs? You have the choice of talking voluntarily or having me wring your neck like a chicken's." Jules voice was calm and low, but he left no doubt in the man's mind that he would carry out his threat.

"I'll talk!" the man squeaked quickly. "Don't wring my neck, please don't. This is only a job to me, I really don't have anything to do with running it. Honest, comrade, you've got to believe that."

"Should we believe him?" Jules asked his sister.

"I think so," she answered coolly. "They wouldn't have picked anyone *this* cowardly to be in charge of anything more demanding than pouring a drink."

"Okay, we believe you," Jules told the fellow. "But you still haven't told us what we want to hear." His grip on the other's neck tightened perceptibly.

"It's all run from that board there, really it is. The whole works!"

"I think he may actually be telling the truth," Yvette said. "There's a whole row of special red indicators that doesn't belong on any PBX unit I've ever seen. Looks like the boss rings down and they set the traps from the board here."

"That's it, that's it!" the bartender burbled, hoping to impress his captors with his helpfulness. "There are blacklight beams and pressure plates across the halls up there, set to trigger blasters or stunners. The boss can call down and the man on the board sets up whatever is ordered, or else I can signal from the bar and everything is set automatically. You didn't give me time to signal, though, so Hans didn't have time to set anything up."

Jules loosened his grip a little, and the man twisted his neck around to keep it from getting stiff. *"Khorosho,"* Jules said. "Now, what's the boss's door like—wood or steel? Locked? And what about guards up there?"

"It's wood. Unlocked, too. No guards—no trouble has ever gotten that far before. The boobytraps in the hallways have always worked before. Hans would've set them, of course, but . . ." His voice trailed off as he looked down again at his friend's still-smoldering remains.

"I believe you, comrade," Jules said, taking his hands completely away from the other's throat. "And to show you how much we trust you, we're going to let you lead the way up to your boss's office. That way, if there are any little surprises waiting for us, you'll be the first to know about them. You're *sure* you've told us everything?"

"Everything I know about it," the man hastened to say.

"Then lead on."

The two d'Alemberts followed the barkeep up the stairs, blasters drawn and at the ready. The man was so nervous he was quivering and could not walk terribly fast—but he did speed up at Jules' prodding. The upper floor, they noticed, was soundproof. All the better; the boss would not have heard the fighting that went on downstairs a short while before.

Nothing happened until the bartender came to a stop in front of one particular door. At Jules' insistence he knocked —no code, just a couple of sharp raps. A voice from inside the room called, "Come in," whereupon they did— quickly, and with their blasters drawn and ready.

The room was not big, but it was comfortably appointed with luxuriant furniture and a broad solentawood desk. The man behind the desk—of medium height, balding, and tending to fat—was alone in the room. He gasped in surprise at the invasion of his inner sanctum and reached for a row of buttons on the desktop, but stopped the motion halfway as Jules' blaster burned a hole through the surface of the desk just centimeters away from his hand.

"Go ahead, push 'em," Jules dared, but the boss remained transfixed, motionless but for the fear-induced quiverings of his muscles.

Jules turned his blaster on the bartender while Yvette stepped forward toward the desk. She kept her blaster aimed at the boss with one hand while with the other she reached into her pocket and pulled out a small hypodermic kit. The hypo was already filled, and she squirted out a little of the clear fluid inside to get rid of any air bubbles.

The man's eyes widened in fear as Yvette approached him. "Not that—*please* not nitrobarb!" he pleaded desperately. "I'm allergic to the stuff—it'll kill me sure, my doctor says."

"What makes you think this is nitrobarb?" Yvette asked innocently. "Nitrobarb's illegal, you know. This could be just plain distilled water."

For some reason, the man did not believe that. "Don't juice me, comrades. I think I probably know what you want . . . and you don't need to give me *anything*! I'll tell you everything I know without it, *honest* I will!"

"Isn't it remarkable how cooperative these people are on Aston?" Jules observed to his sister.

True to his word, the crime boss babbled out everything he knew about the entire organization on Aston and elsewhere. Jules taped every single word on the minirecorder he carried, to pass on eventually to the local Service officials. The organizational structure here was quite similar to that on Algonia, except that the man at the top was not of the nobility; but the man's story did have one significant addition—word about shipments of stolen arms between planets. Thousands of smuggled guns and blaster cannons were traveling through the spaceways from point A to point B. The d'Alemberts' guesses about a secret army were that much closer to being confirmed—and *that* meant that Banion, or whoever else was behind this conspiracy, was preparing to act soon.

When the man got around to listing his own boss, the trail, as Jules had expected—pointed clearly and unmistakably to one reclusive man living in a big, lonely mansion outside the capital city of the planet Durward.

"See," Jules said when the crime boss had finished, "isn't everything so much more pleasant when you cooperate with us? Just because you've been so helpful we'll even let you live. After all, a traitor whom you know is no real threat. You'll be watched, of course, and maybe arrested if the local chief decides to, but you'll probably live." Turning to his sister, he said, "I suppose our next move is to Durward."

"That's where the action seems to be," she replied. "But we'd better go in armed to the teeth—that house won't be easy to crack. Fortunately, we've got some equipment they've never even heard of."

They tied their two captives up and headed back downstairs. "Do you think we laid it on thickly enough for them?" Jules wondered aloud.

"Undoubtedly. As soon as they get loose—and we tied those ropes pretty sloppily—they'll be reporting everything to whoever the contact man is on Durward."

Gathering up their six relatives, the d'Alembert party moved back to the spaceport, where Jules and Yvette were in for a pleasant surprise. Rick and his team had come to Aston in one of the large transport ships the Circus used for heavy moving—and one of the items that had been fitted into the hold was Jules' and Yvette's own two-person subspacer, *La Comète Cuivré*. They were delighted to see the ship, because now they could give it its first official use —and because it would get them back to Earth faster than the big, bulky freighter the others had come in.

They said farewell to their relatives and spent the rest of the evening and night inside the *Comet*'s control room— the most secure spot they could find on the planet. They occupied their time encoding and transmitting a report to the Head on all they had uncovered here and saying that they would be returning to Earth directly; but they did not mention their suspicions about grand ducal involvement. Better not to cast aspersions until they had a few more facts to go on.

When that was done, Jules rose, stretched and walked over to the galactic chart. His eyes brooding, he set it for maximum span and turned on the activating circuits. As the great wispy star clouds of the galactic lens took form, each surveyed star positioned with minute accuracy, he keyed the index locators for Durward—the planet to which all their hard-earned information pointed so surely—and then for Earth. Quickly the taped data spools whined and spun and printed out course and the dizzying distance in parsecs

110

between the two planets. "Every single clue we've seen," he said slowly, "points directly and unequivocally to Durward as the spot where the action is . . ."

"I know, Julie," said his sister, covering a yawn. "So of course we're going to Earth. Well, what are we waiting for?"

Another green dot turned to blue, thought the tall, thin man as he angrily crumpled the report he'd just read on the Aston fiasco. *Another planet lost, for the time being.* He still had plenty, so the loss was not critical, but nevertheless . . . nevertheless, this slow, tiny erosion was annoying.

A follow-up report indicated that most of the gang on Aston had been picked up by the local branch of SOTE and would probably receive prison sentences. *Serves them right for being so incompetent,* he thought, then turned his attention to the matter of the special SOTE team of agents.

They had shown themselves to be terribly resourceful in their first two attempts, but of course they were bound to fail now. The entire planet of Durward was filled with boobytraps, ready to spring on any agents who came looking for him there. No, now that they were heading for Durward he could dismiss them utterly from his mind and concentrate on the real problem—the fleet strategies for his upcoming naval uprising against the Crown. But even that would have to wait a moment, as the chiming of his clock reminded him that it was time for his appointment with his physical fitness counselor.

Had he known that the two agents were heading toward Earth rather than Durward, he might have spent a few more minutes contemplating their identity and their fate. But, confident of his boobytraps, he proceeded on to his appointment without another thought given to those two determined operatives.

CHAPTER 12

The Massagerie

The planet Earth, as was only proper, became the seat of Imperial government. Moscow was chosen as the site for the principal Imperial Palace, with subsidiary palaces in New York, London, Tokyo, Buenos Aires and Los Angeles. Imperial court took place at any of these locales, but the administration of the Empire was a business that occupied nearly a third of Earth's population either directly or indirectly. Because of the fact of Earth's central position in the Empire, the various nobles of Earth held far more actual power than their titles indicated. The counts of Moskva and Los Angeles, for example, held more real power than most earls and marquises; more power, even, than a great number of dukes. (Manley, Traces of Royalty, slot 176.)

Jules and Yvette had no sooner arrived back on Earth than they found a message waiting for them, along with any number of reels of computer output. The Service accountants had completed their financial survey of galactic trends, and the results were all ready to be analyzed. Rolling up their figurative sleeves, the pair dug in and started the monumental task.

Three days later, certain trends were beginning to make themselves evident. Through eyes made bleary by fatigue and staring at too many numbers, the d'Alemberts looked at the graphs they had drawn and began making some conclusions. "It looks fairly certain," Jules said wearily, "that there are unaccounted influxes of cash in Sectors Two, Thirteen, Twenty, Twenty-Two and Thirty-Five. The money just disappears once it goes in there, as though they were dumping it in a hole."

"Or a secret army," Yvette pointed out.

"That is the more logical guess. Thirteen and Twenty, in particular, are the big gainers. I find it interesting that Durward, which is in Sector Ten, shows no unusual cash problems whatsover."

"Confirming your guess that it's only a decoy."

Jules shrugged. "Perhaps. At any rate, we now have some new facts to play around with. Let's see what we can do with them."

They requested—and got—the complete dossiers on the rulers of each of the suspicious sectors and their families. Another whole day was spent going over these records, then they had another conference.

"Every one of them is beyond reproach," Yvette said dejectedly. "Not a single scandal has marked any of those families for at least a hundred years. If Banion is involved with any of them, he's managed to keep himself squeaky clean for quite a while."

"He would, of course. He'd do everything in his power to escape detection until he's ready to make his move. Even so much as a traffic ticket could bring him to the attention of the Service's computers. But I'm more convinced than ever that the person we're looking for is somewhere within that group."

"Swell, but how do we narrow the field? As I said before, we can't just go around sticking nitrobarb into grand dukes until we find the right one."

Jules considered the problem. "The only way," he said, "is to get to know them better, get ourselves in a position of trust that we can work from."

"There's only two of us, so we can't hire out as servants to all our suspects."

"*Khorosho,* then we find some service that we can perform for all of them equally. What's faddish in the Upper Court this year?"

"Physical fitness, from what I read on the newsrolls. Everybody and his noble brother has a private gym and a personal instructor to keep him from getting too flabby. Being in top condition has become an obsession in the higher echelons. Of course, we were into it before it became stylish."

"I'd say that's just about perfect for us. It'll let us get close to them without their realizing what we're up to."

"But how will we make them come to us?"

"Make them?" Jules smiled. "They'll consider themselves lucky if we *let* them!"

One month later, safe within the confines of his private office, the Head was talking to a tall, thin man with graying hair who, while old, was in no sense decrepit. Duchess Helena sat across the room with her shapely legs crossed, sipping nonchalantly at a cream liqueur while her father and his friend talked.

"I'm afraid they've even got *me* confused, Zan," the older man said. "What can it all mean? Under no circumstances is the Circus to go to Durward, they say, and preferably it's to remain here on extended performance. That's easy enough to arrange, it's a popular enough attraction. Carlos and Carmen Velasquez are not to report in, they say, and nothing that pair does, however wild, will be of any importance. That's fine, too. But what is the meaning of this *beauty* parlor business right here on Earth? It doesn't make sense!"

"Not a beauty parlor, Bill," the Head said quietly. "A massagerie deluxe. Or rather, 'The House of Strength of Body and of Heart.' "

"Little difference. Do *you* at least know what they're doing?"

"Very little; and what's more, I don't particularly want to know. They're the top people I have . . ."

"*Potentially*," the other pointed out. "Remember, the thousand point test only measures potential. They've never had field experience on any case this major before."

"Well, if they can't handle it we might as well surrender now. I haven't got anybody more qualified on hand at the moment."

"I think Jules d'Alembert could handle anything," Helena said quietly from her corner, but her remark went unnoticed by the two men.

"I think I may have been a little too supervisorial on this matter before," the Head continued. "Having the boss constantly peering over his shoulder tends to distract an agent and discourage initiative. I've given them this job and their father's given them their training; the rest is up to them. Besides," he added significantly, "while I *think* I've weeded all the traitors out of the office here, I don't know for sure. Too much contact with them might break their cover."

114

"A good point," the older man nodded.

"I would hazard a guess that they have some particular suspect or suspects in mind who would be likely to take an interest in body building. This, you will note, implies that they have reached the stage where they can narrow their attention to individuals . . . I don't know who they have in mind, but I consider it a hopeful sign."

"But staying so far away from Durward . . ."

"May be the best thing they can do. So many good agents have already died there that it might just be a trap. Anyway, as long as the d'Alemberts are working on this case I'll give them anything they want, no questions asked."

"That's only right, especially since they want so little from us. I still find it hard to believe that they don't ask us for expenses. I know the Circus' taxes are rebated, but surely they spend more than that on Empire business."

"My guess is, they don't. The Velasquez couple is a large outlay, certainly, but they frequently counter it with cheaper disguises. And the Circus is so successful that its taxes are ridiculously high. The Duke won't tell me *how* high, of course—he's a funny man that way. I asked him once if we didn't owe him some money, and he told me if I wanted to count kopeks I should get myself a job in a grocery store."

The old man laughed. "That sounds just like him, all right. But DesPlaines is a rich planet, you know, and Etienne d'Alembert is a tremendously able man—as well as being one of my best friends. Well, I'd better leave you to your work now. I like talking to you when I'm feeling low, Zan; you give me a lift." He raised his nearly-empty glass and gave the Service salute: "Tomorrow, fellow and friend. May we all live to see it."

"When they finished drinking the toast, His Imperial Majesty William Stanley, Tenth Emperor of the Empire of Earth and all human domains, rose to his feet and walked majestically out of the room.

Helena grinned up at her father. "You didn't exactly lie, I know; but if he knew as much as we do I bet he wouldn't feel so uplifted."

"He has troubles enough of his own without having to worry about ours—or about the loyalty of his own grand dukes. Besides, we don't know yet who's behind it. It could be someone outside their five suspects, just as easily as not."

"Do you really think so?"

The Head turned away. "I don't know. I've known each of them for years. That's another reason why I want to stay out of the d'Alemberts' way; I don't want my personal feelings to influence the case."

The girl got up from her chair, walked across the room and began massaging the back of her father's neck tenderly. "If we had even a good suspicion, he'd get a shot of nitrobarb," she said. "But all we've got on paper is a suspicious flow of cash into some places where it shouldn't be. That's not enough evidence to convict a cockroach, let alone a grand duke before the High Court of Justice. But how under the sun and moon and eleven circumpolar stars can this glorified gymnasium help solve the puzzle?"

"I haven't even the most tenuous idea, my dear—and just between us two, I'm as curious about it as you are."

A ten-story gravity-controlled building in the Mytishchi district of the sprawling urban complex that was modern Moscow had been remodeled from top to bottom. All the work had been done by the high-grav personnel who now occupied the building. The facade, now three stories high with marble statues of Atlas serving as pillars on either side of the immense doors, was topped by a triple-tube brilliant sign that flared its red light into the open air:

DANGER—THREE GRAVITIES—DANGER

On each side of those monstrous portals, in small, severely plain obsidian letters on a silver background, a plaque read:

duClos

The prepublicity campaign for this health spa had been as successful as it was subtle. For weeks before the opening, the rumor had spread softly through the upper strata of the court that this House of Strength would cater only to the topmost flakes of the upper crust—and that was precisely what it did. Applicants, even from the nobility, were turned down by the scores. Its first clients—and for a week its only clients—were the extremely powerful Count of Moskva, his Countess and their two gangling teenage daughters. Since this display of ultra-snobbishness appealed very strongly to the ultra-snobbishness of the high nobility of the Capital of Empire, "duClos" raised snobbery to heights seldom attained anywhere in history.

After the first week, pressures became very great, and the House of Strength of Body and of Heart "relaxed" its standards the merest bit and admitted two grand dukes and their families—neither of whom were suspected of participating in the Banion matter in any way. The fees charged for these personal services were literally astronomical, but none of the customers complained; they were really getting their money's worth, though they would hardly have guessed that the man working on improving their bodies was actually *the* best male athlete in the Empire.

The d'Alemberts had decided between them that Yvette should stay pretty much out of sight this time around. The opposition would be on the lookout for a team of Des-Plainians; if Jules appeared to be alone, it would allay any suspicions they might have about him. So the distaff member of the pair had once more gone into disguise—one of the more difficult she'd ever done, for it is hard on anyone—particularly a young, attractive person like Yvette—to *intentionally* make herself less attractive than she really was. Yet that was what she had done. She added lines to her face and padded her cheeks out to make herself appear twenty years older. Her clothes, while chic, were more matronly in fashion and gave her a slightly dowdy appearance. She wore her hair in an unbecoming bun and became Gospozha Henrietta Bergere, the middle-aged appointments secretary and assistant to duClos.

One night in the middle of the third week of operations, Jules came out to his sister's desk after the rest of the staff had gone home. "How're you doing, sis?"

"I'm being bored out of my skull," she replied. "Of all the deadly situations I've ever been in, the worst is being ennuied to death. Give me an army of angry mobsters with blazing blasters, any time; this desk jockeying'll put me in an early grave. Any luck with the case?"

"A few bites here and there, but nothing solid. But the more I think about it, the more likely Sector Twenty looks to me."

"In that case, let me clue you in on something I've been mulling over for a few days. I wasn't going to mention it until I could thicken it up a bit, but since you brought the subject up, how does this sound? You know that Duchess of Swingleton, the snooty little jamtart who's supposed to be the daughter of Grand Duchess Olga of Sector Twenty?"

Jules raised an eyebrow. *"Supposed* to be?"

"Well, is then," Yvette laughed. "Maybe I shouldn't have put it quite that way, but I've gotten so used to sneering at nobility these last few weeks that it comes out naturally now—in my own inimitable ladylike fashion, of course."

"I wouldn't put *that* 'quite that way,' either. If it were me on the receiving end of that sneer I'd use my fist on you as a dental drill."

"Duchess Tanya certainly would like to, if she dared. I've been giving her the royal snoot all along, and she's burning like a torch. Her mother takes the whole thing in stride, but little Tanya is acting as though our snubbing her were a royal affront."

"You and I have both known a lot of spoiled little noble brats who act that way at the drop of a hat."

"Perhaps; but the thought keeps crossing my mind that perhaps this girl knows she may be in line to inherit far more than Sector Twenty if the solar wind blows the right way."

Jules stiffened. "You're implying, then, that she may be the Bastard's daughter?"

"I'm implying that we should check her out, since she could be a weak link in the chain."

"All right, refresh me on her dossier."

"Only child of Grand Duke Nicholas Otamar and Grand Duchess Olga of Sector Twenty, so she stands to inherit a good deal right there; ultra-beautiful; was married at age nineteen to Duke Titos Boros of Swingleton, who was eighty-nine at the time. Suffice it to say that two years later, Duke Titos departed our spiritual plane, leaving the planet Swingleton to his daughter by a previous marriage—and leaving Tanya Boros, nee Otamar, with the title of Dowager Duchess at age twenty-one. That was four years ago, and she's made no attempt to change her status in the meantime."

"And you think she's taking your insults a little too seriously for a dowager duchess? Perhaps. But if she's only twenty-five now, wouldn't that make her a bit young to be the Bastard's daughter?"

"Maybe *you* plan to get senile at an early age, but it doesn't affect most men. Look at our Emperor, for example. He's only a year younger than the Bastard would be now, and he's got a daughter who's twenty-three."

"Point noted and well taken," Jules admitted.

"All I'm saying," Yvette elucidated, "is that if she is Banion's daughter, she seems to be the perfect way to attack. She has so many soft spots she'd make an ideal target."

"Yes, it might be interesting to attack her soft spots."

"Wipe that grin off your face, you lecherous brute, or I'll report you to Vonnie. Duchess Tanya is beautiful, athletic, rich, talented, noble and spoiled rotten. She's emotionally retarded, too, with the maturity level of a fifteen year old. Her hobby—or perhaps I should say her avocation— is men, and she works hard at it. She's about as choosy as an alley cat, which is an apt description even if I do say so myself. So my thought is this: if we can give her the idea that Gospodin duClos is the guiding force behind the House of Strength I'm positive she'll redouble her efforts to get you to coach her yourself—personally. You, of course, give in with great reluctance, but instead of bowing down and worshipping her like the other men do, you act like —and even say that—you wouldn't be caught dead with her at a catfight, to say nothing of in bed. If I'm right, she could blow up like a bomb and let slip with something she shouldn't say."

"All right," Jules said with a smile and a shrug. "I just hope Vonnie appreciates all the sacrifices I make for her."

Three days later, Jules accompanied Yvette to the four-story mansion that served as home to the Dowager Duchess of Swingleton. The large house was staffed by a dozen servants—all except two being lusty young men—and was furnished in lavish decadence. Brocade draperies in deep rose shades enhanced the walls, while plush pink carpeting underfoot made walking an absolute pleasure. The furniture was upholstered in wine-colored velvet and thickly padded for maximum comfort.

The Duchess Tanya reclined on a divan at the far end of the room. She was a tall girl—at least ten centimeters taller than Jules—and as beautiful as a Grecian statue come to life. She wore a silver lamé dress that accentuated every line of her body. A mass of platinum-colored hair was arranged high upon a proudly held head. Her face had a

119

look of self-indulgence about it, but there was a gleam of intelligence shining behind those dark blue eyes as she watched Jules enter. A predatory smile tickled the corners of her lips.

After Yvette formally presented him, Jules walked slowly around the divan once, studying the Duchess's form from every possible angle. Finally he scowled and said, *"Maybe I can do something with this, but there doesn't seem to be much of anything there to work with. Peel, girl, and I'll see."*

"Peel?" The girl's head went even higher, her eyes blazed with cold indignation. "Are you talking to *me?*" she flared.

"I'm talking to a mass of fat and a little flabby meat that ought to be muscle but isn't," he replied caustically. "Do you expect a master sculptor to make something of a tub of clay without touching it? If you are burdened with modesty, I suppose you could wear a bikini or tights— although how you can imagine that I, duClos, would become sexually aroused over such a slug's body as yours is completely beyond my comprehension."

"Get out!" Trembling with rage, she pointed at the door. "Leave my home at once!"

He gave her his choicest, top-deck sneer. "Madame, nothing could possibly please me more. I detest making house calls in this abominably weak field you consider gravity, and was only prevailed upon to do so by my secretary, who assured me that you would make an ideal client." He turned to glare at Yvette. "I see I shall have to have some words with her upon my return." With that, he spun on his heel and walked coldly toward the door.

"Wait, you! Turn around!"

• Jules stopped and slowly turned, making certain that the sneer was still engraved on his features. "Yes?"

"I will remind you that I am the Dowager Duchess of Swingleton, one of the richest planets in Sector Twenty!"

"And I will remind you, madame, that I am duClos. There are hundreds upon hundreds of duchesses and dowagers, but there is only one duClos. I am unique."

Jules could see that the fiery young girl was struggling to control her temper and, after a second, that anger had been banked. "Wait, then," she said. "I'll put on a swimsuit. After all, I *do* want to find out whether you're any good or not."

She left the room for five minutes, but when she came back—dressed in twenty centimeters worth of fabric more than nothing—duClos was even less impressed with her physique than before. "Lard," he muttered as his talented fingers objectively explored nearly every square centimeter of her body. "Flabby, unrendered lard. It will be a great challenge, to be sure, but duClos is equal to the task. I am told you have your own gymnasium within your house; take me to it."

"Why, aren't we going to your place?"

He looked at her in amused and condescending surprise. "Are you *that* stupid. You'd fall flat and could barely get up, because you'd be carrying the weight of two other dowager duchesses as well as your own. The titles alone would be too heavy for you. It'll take a month of work here before you'll be able to enter the House of Strength. To your gymnasium, I say. *Vite, vite!*"

The Duchess reluctantly led Jules and Yvette to her gym, which was as fully equipped as could be expected for an amateur set-up. "First," Jules said, stripping to his shorts, "I shall show you what we accustomed to three Earth gravities can do easily here on Earth." He then proceeded to go through a routine of such vigor and violence that the apparatus creaked and groaned, and the very floor of the room shook. In spite of herself, the Duchess applauded when he was done.

"Now," said Jules, acknowledging her applause graciously, "I shall show you what a fair Earth gymnast—such as perhaps I'll be able to make out of you—can do," and he demonstrated that, as well. Duchess Tanya, who'd thought she kept herself in pretty good condition, was frankly astonished.

"Now I'll find out what you can do—if anything. Let me see fifty fast push-ups, right now." The Duchess tried gamely, but made it only to twenty-seven before her arms gave out and she collapsed onto the mat. Jules scowled over her, a sight that both frightened and enraged her. She swore to herself that she would never give him the occasion to sneer at her again if she could help it.

Jules worked unmercifully for half an hour, which was about all she could have taken. To her credit, Jules noted that she did not complain once, no matter how harshly he treated her. Finally he said, "That's enough for today, poor

121

thing." Then, turning to Yvette, said, "Give her a massage in steam, and go deep. After that, the usual."

"No," the girl said between pants as she recovered her breath from the last exercise. "I want you to do it yourself. They say you're the tops, and I want nothing but the best."

Jules pretended to consider that. "Perhaps that would be best," he announced. "That way I will be able to tell more exactly how well you are developing. *Alors,* let us proceed to the steamroom."

The Duchess was careful to have her maidservant present in the steamroom to act as chaperone. She needn't have bothered. Although the serving girl was shocked—or pretended to be—at the idea of a three-quarters naked man working his hands over the body of her completely naked mistress, Jules was the only one in the room who was, apparently, unaffected by the entire process. He was merely an expert masseur working at his profession, nothing more.

This procedure went on daily for about a week. Jules now left Yvette back at the office because, as he said, "I think I can get further along with her if you're not around to inhibit her."

"I'll bet," Yvette winked at him, even though she knew Jules considered the lovely Duchess a duty and nothing else.

Since the Duchess was actually a strong, healthy, athletic girl, splendidly built and agile both physically and mentally—despite duClos' derision—she learned fast and developed fast. But for the first time in her life, she had struck a man and bounced. He seemed disinterested in either her title or her manifest physical charms. It was, to her, an intolerable situation—and a situation that got no better at all as time and their relationship progressed.

Even after more than two weeks he stayed coldly impersonal and more than somewhat contemptuous. He was, and he remained, a master wasting his talents on material entirely unworthy of his skill. He paid no attention whatsoever to any of the little flirtatious ploys she made in his direction.

One day, however, when she had become a pretty fair gymnast and was very proud of her accomplishments, her maidservant disappeared before the massage was to begin. "We don't need her any more, I don't think," she said softly. Lying back on the massage table with her wispy garment draped only loosely over her breasts, she shot him a seductive glance calculated to arouse even a statue to passion. "Do we?"

It is an enormous tribute to Jules' nobler instincts—and to his love for his darling Vonnie—that he was able to conquer the basic animal urges that were coursing through his body at that moment. "I don't, that's for sure," he said with his familiar sneer. That expression had become so maddening to her over the past few weeks that she wanted to bash it back into his skull with a sledgehammer. "And if you are trying to seduce me you're wasting your time. You are a lump of unfinished plasticine that I am trying to mold into something halfway worthwhile. You mean nothing else to me. I'd no more consider intimacy with you than with any other warm mass of poor-grade clay—or ten kopeks' worth of catmeat, for that matter."

That did the trick admirably. The Dowager Duchess's temper blew sky high, and the fire in her eyes could have melted steel. "You clod!" she screamed. "You common oaf! You base-born peasant! I should have you staked out and flayed alive for treason like that. I could . . ." She stopped her screaming suddenly and her eyes widened just the tiniest bit. The expression in them was unreadable.

"Quiet, creature!" he snapped back at her, timing his interruption so perfectly that she *knew* he could not have been paying attention to what she'd been saying. "My birth, high or low, has no bearing in this matter. I am duClos. I am trying to mold you into what our Creator intended you to be: His instrument to beget *men,* not the milksops and flabs currently infesting this sinful planet Earth."

"Oh? Don't tell me you're a *Puritan!*" she exclaimed, very glad indeed to change the subject. Her outburst of anger was almost completely forgotten. "I should have known it, though, by all that hair."

"An ex-Puritan," he corrected her. "I differ from my former colleagues in that I don't believe that everything pleasant is sinful. But neglect of that Divine instrument known as the human body most certainly is. Lie back and I shall continue the massage. I will ignore your display of temper, provided it does not happen again, in the light of the progress you have made to date."

Work went on, exactly as though nothing had happened. Four days later she graduated into the House of

Strength itself, doing as well there as could be expected from a native of a one-gee planet.

And she managed to convince herself, quite easily, that she had not revealed any hint of the secret that had been held silent for sixty-seven years.

CHAPTER 13

The Fortress of Englewood

As an example of the traditional loyalty of the Navy: When Empress Stanley Five, her husband and four of their five children were assassinated in 2299 their youngest child, Prince Edward, escaped death only because he, then an ensign in the Navy, was being guarded as no other person had ever been guarded before. Fleet Admiral Simms—who ironically had performed the same service for Edward's mother nine years earlier—declared martial law and, in the bloodiest purge in all recorded history, executed not only all those found guilty—including the late Empress's brother and sister-in-law—but also their entire families for good measure. He then made himself regent and ruled with an iron hand for six years. Then, to the vast surprise of all (and the relief of many), he relinquished his regency on the day that Prince Edward came of age. It was he himself who crowned the young prince Emperor Stanley Six. (Farnham, The Empire, Reel 2, slot 784.)

"You're positive she said 'treason'?" Yvette reiterated. They couldn't afford any slipups at this stage of the game.

"I couldn't have missed a word like that, Evie."

Both of them knew what the Duchess's use of that word meant. The crime of treason was an act against either the Empire or the Emperor. Crimes against the lesser nobility were considered civil crimes, and tried accordingly. For Duchess Tanya to accuse duClos of treason meant that she considered herself to be of Imperial rank. And, since there was no known Stanley blood in her heritage, there was only one place she could have gotten such a lineage—from Banion the Bastard.

"We can't hang her on the basis of that one word, you know."

"No," Jules admitted, "but it gives us the wedge we need. We now know where to look—and if we look hard enough we'll find what we want. Nobody can cover their trail that completely."

He paused. "Damn it, and I was just starting to like that girl, too. She was almost behaving herself."

"Save your sympathy," Yvette said coldly. "If she's not executed outright for treason, she'll certainly be banished to Gastonia for her complicity in the matter."

"I know, I know. Hand me her father's file, will you?" He took the reel Yvette handed him and fed it through the viewer. "Grand Duke Nicholas Otamar. Born a commoner in 2382, according to the birth certificate listed here; that would make him two years younger than Banion is supposed to be."

"Birth certificates can be forged," Yvette said distractedly. Her mind seemed to be on something else.

"And something that long ago would be almost impossible to verify now," Jules agreed. "Usual school records and such. He gained his current title by marrying Grand Duchess Olga Ferensky in 2410. That's kind of unusual, for a grand duchess to marry a commoner. Not impossible, of course, but it would certainly have helped him woo her if he could have shown her the Patent of Royalty his mother hid away for him . . ."

"That's it!" Yvette shouted suddenly, slapping her palm down hard on the table in front of her. Her action was so abrupt that Jules jumped involuntarily.

"What's what?" he asked.

"A piece just clicked into place. We get so used to calling nobility by title, first name and territory that we usually ignore the last name. Papa, for instance, is usually just called Duke Etienne of DesPlaines; the d'Alembert is understood. We've been calling this guy Grand Duke Nicholas of Twenty so long that we've totally missed the point of his last name!"

"Otamar?"

"Don't you see? It's an anagram of 'Amorat.' Aimée Amorat, the Bastard's mother."

Jules now pounded his own fist on the table. "Eve, you've nailed him. He's got to be our man." He turned the reel in the viewer to a picture of Grand Duke Nicholas and stared

126

hard at the man's face. "You know, now that we know his identity for a fact, you can see the Stanley lineage in his face. Long and angular, sort of squared-off chin behind that goatee of his, the same bushy eyebrows . . ."

"We don't know it for a fact, though," Yvette reminded him. "All we have is one wrong word from his daughter and a name that could be an anagram. If the Head is going to present this case to the Emperor, he'll need a lot more substantial evidence—he'll need the Patent itself."

"And we'll get it for him," Jules said with determination. "Now that we know who's got it, it's only a matter of time."

DuClos deigned to accept six grand dukes and duchesses as personal clients—among them Grand Duke Nicholas and Grand Duchess Olga of Sector Twenty—but that was all he would take. Working from that position of intimacy, Jules tried to delve deeper into the private affairs of that two-some, but to no avail. Their public facades passed the closest scrutiny.

Yvette tried working from a slightly different direction. Since Nicholas and Olga maintained three estates on Earth, each with a large staff, the turnover of their personnel was quite high. At every opportunity, Yvette managed to wangle one of her family members into those households—in kitchens, garages, and anyplace else—in an effort to find the slightest traces of information. Little bits and pieces manifested themselves—strange cryptic messages arriving at odd hours, an unusual assortment of people visiting the Grand Duke, and so forth—but there was nothing to prove that Nicholas was indeed Banion, that Nicholas was planning an imminent revolt, or that Nicholas had possession of the all-important Patent of Royalty.

"We've *got* to take this to the Head, Eve," Jules said at last, after several more weeks of fruitless searching. "I hate to yell for help on our first really big job, but Nicholas is just too fat a cat for us to tackle on our own. If we make even the slightest goof, there's more than a possibility that it'd be the Head's head that would roll, not Nicholas'. We simply *can't* take that risk by ourselves."

Yvette nodded. "You're right, I'm afraid. The Emperor himself sits in judgment at any trial of a grand duke, and he'd be a fair judge even in a matter like this. If we can't conclusively *prove* Nicholas guilty of treason, the Emperor would let him go."

They met the next day with the Head and laid the whole mess out before him as clearly and concisely as they could. As they spoke, they could see him aging ten years; and when they were done he sat silent and motionless, in intense concentration, for a full ten minutes. Neither d'Alembert spoke another word while he was so engrossed. In the hushed atmosphere they could almost hear the master strategist's keen brain at work.

"Nicholas," he whispered at last, as though to himself. "I can't say I'm shocked, particularly; but even so, I've known the man for years. We weren't especially close, but he was polite enough company at some awfully tedious state banquets."

He laid his hands out flat, palms down, in front of him and looked up at his two top agents. "You're both right, of course—we can't move against *him* without the genuine Patent actually in our hands."

Jules scowled. "That's what I was afraid you'd say. And I'm sure that Patent must be in the solidest safe-deposit vault on Earth."

"It isn't," the Head said flatly. "The Emperor can open any bank vault he pleases, with no reasons or excuses at all. Nicholas knows that. Besides, he wouldn't want that Patent anywhere out of his immediate grasp, and who knows what could happen to it in some bank? So the Patent's got to be in a vault as good as any on Earth, but probably one in the deepest subcellar of his Castle Englewood. I'd stake my head on that. In fact," he added, enjoying the irony, "I undoubtedly will.

"Theoretically, the Emperor could open even a grand duke's personal vaults, too, at whim. But the legal machinery grinding into action would tip our hand, and probably spur the Bastard to precipitate revolt. Nicholas' army and navy are of unknown strength; once he got them mobilized, who knows which side would win? At the very least, we would face a bloody civil war that would claim billions of lives on hundreds of worlds, and the scars would be with us for generations.

"No, gentleman and lady, we are all going to have to stake our heads on this gamble. No matter how daintily we pussyfoot it, there's always the chance of our touching off the explosion. We might as well all go out in style.

"Now, as to the ways and means. At the slightest hint of trouble, Nicholas would try to kill the Emperor and establish his claim, so we'll have to get Bill out of the way. Edna is a safer target, since there'd be little gained by killing the Crown Princess while her father is still alive. What do you think of this?" and they discussed details for two hours.

Three days later, the various news media announced that Emperor Stanley Ten had had a heart attack.

It wasn't too serious as those things went, they hastened to point out, but a battery of medical specialists agreed unanimously that he had to have at least two months of carefree rest—preferably at his favorite summer place, Big Piney in the Rocky Mountains. Wherefore Crown Princess Edna was given the most unusual title of "Empress Pro Tem" and her parents departed the Imperial Palace with no pomp or circumstance at all. They did not go to Big Piney, however, but to a specially selected island in the Pacific that was guarded by every defensive device known to the military science of the age. And, just coincidentally, a small but able fleet of battle cruisers hovered in synchronous orbit over that spot to guard against a concerted attack from space.

Meanwhile, to relieve the concern in the minds of the Empire's subjects, Empress Pro Tem Edna announced a Grand Ball—a getting-acquainted party that, beginning with a full Grand Imperial Court, would last for three days. All thirty-six grand dukes and grand duchesses and their families were invited, as well as all the nobles of Earth above the rank of count and any visiting nobles from out in space. There was, of course, no chance that any of the invitees would turn down such an event, which promised to be the social climax of the decade.

With the cat away, the mice set out to very serious work indeed. Castle Englewood appeared from the outside to be deserted except for the servants who managed the estate. Jules and Yvette invaded the castle with a small army of both relatives and technical experts. The staff—some of than they had any right to be—were overpowered without than they had any right to me—were overpowered without too much fuss. Fifty cat-footed, fully briefed d'Alembert wrestlers were quite sufficient to take care of even the many-times-too-numerous Castle Guard. Once the help was dispatched, the Service people had free run of the castle—theoretically.

Architects and engineers had brought along the detailed blueprints of the castle, as registered with the Imperial Building Commission but, as had been expected, the plans were found useless. Most of the actual details that mattered had never been registered. So the Service's best electronic wizards moved in, unlimbered their ultrasensitive detectors and explored walls, floors and ceilings. They traced cable after cable, wire after wire; and as they traced, they figured out what each system was and cut it. Section after section of the vast castle went dark and powerless as these experts went through, skirting the defenses and dismantling the traps.

Eventually, after more than three hours of grueling, mind-numbing detail work, they found the Grand Duke's personal elevator tube. Riding it down to the subbasement, they found the enormous scale model of the Empire with its various colored lights still twinkling. The sight was awesome, and it forged one more damning link in the chain, but it still was not enough. They *had* to find that Patent.

It had, of course, been obvious from the start that Castle Englewood was no ordinary grand ducal residence. The invaders from SOTE found it a fortress; a fortress that, except for the Head's brilliant strategy of deception and the d'Alemberts' ability to carry it out, would have been starkly impregnable. And, even so, the attack almost failed.

The castle had been searched from top to bottom, with every possible place of concealment pried open and examined. No trace had been found of that all-important document. Finally, after exploring all the other subterranean tunnels and computer banks, Jules and his company returned to a grimly thick steel wall that stood boldly at the end of one broad corridor. "How about this, Major?" Jules asked.

The officer in charge of the military aspects of this raid examined the wall in minute detail. "It opens from somewhere, somehow," he said, pointing out an almost invisible crack where steel butted against steel. "A lot of effort has gone into disguising it, though, so it'd probably take us a week to find out where and how it opens. I *think* we cut all the external leads in, but I'd bet this section has its own independent power source."

"We'll have to assume that, yes," Jules replied. "And

automatic stunners—or worse, blasters. Gas maybe, or triggered bombs. But the Head gambled his life on a lot less than we know now, so bring up your shields and high-powers and burn the damned thing down."

Fortunately, the corridor that led up to this blank wall was a very wide one, fifteen meters from side to side. Heavy armored shields were brought down to protect the assailants from automatic blaster beams. Jules and Yvette and the team of d'Alembert weightlifters and wrestlers—led by their cousin Rick once more—all donned spacesuits to protect them from any gas that might be released. Then they brought into play the special heavy-duty blasters to cut through the wall that faced them.

Slowly, centimeter by centimeter, the unbelievable fury of those beams ate through the twenty-centimeter thick plating in front of them. When the cutting was through, that heavy wall of metal fell inward onto a steel floor, producing a crash that rattled the teeth of the SOTE agents and shook the very bedrock upon which Castle Englewood was built.

The collapse of that wall revealed a brightly-lit room behind it where, seated around a small table, was a squad of ten DesPlainian weightlifters—Grand Duke Nicholas' last line of defense.

One glance was all the attackers had time for, though, because at the same instant that the wall fell everyone in the tunnel—guards and SOTE operatives alike—were yanked to the floor with a force the likes of which none of them had ever experienced before.

"Ultragrav!" Jules gasped as the wind was knocked from his lungs when he hit the smooth floor. And indeed it was; the toppling of the wall had turned on the final protective device, a totally unexpected one. The entire corridor was now experiencing an artificial gravitational field of some twenty-five gravities. Jules and Yvette, who felt quite comfortable at three gees and could get around without too much hindrance at six or seven, were pinned flat to the ground, helpless as babies. They could barely lift a finger to help themselves.

Imminent danger threatened. Their own shield, set up to protect them from blaster fire, now held them in deadly peril. It had not been meant to stand up under such extreme conditions, and was wobbling visibly. If it fell backwards onto them, the people it had been meant to protect

131

would be smashed to a thin layer of ooze on the tunnel floor. "Shield!" Jules gasped out in warning.

Rick had seen the danger, too. Unlike Jules and Yvette, he was a trained wrestler; the muscles in his body had been specially toughened to supernormal strength. Thus, while the ultragrav was crippling to him as well, he was at least able to move. With a feeble lurch, he pushed his body forward against the shield. That one slight push was all that was needed in a gravitational field as strong as this; the armor plating toppled forward with a bang that jolted everyone's bones.

"Nice," Yvette complimented him through gritted teeth. "Now, can you get those other guys before they get us?"

"We're working on it," Rick said hoarsely of his team, and they were.

If the situation had not been life-and-death it would actually have been comic to watch those hundred-and-fifty-kilogram brawlers, each one muscled to put an Atlas to shame, exerting every iota of their tremendous strength to such puny results: first to get up onto their knees and then to lift, using all the strength of both arms, a two kilogram weapon up into some kind of firing position. Unfortunately, one of the Grand Duke's guards—a giant even for a DesPlainian weightlifter—made it before any of the d'Alemberts. His first blast went straight through the man on Jules' left, who had managed to reach his knees. The man screamed and collapsed very quickly.

The next blast hit Jules, who was still pinned flat, just below his left knee. He screamed with agony as a fist-sized chunk of skin was burned out of his calf, then passed out completely from the pain. The blood, being pulled out of the wound by a force many times stronger than normal, flowed copiously.

Yvette watched her brother's injury with horror, and reacted as quickly as she could under the circumstances. Within a field of twenty-five gees, the blood would be drained from even a small wound very rapidly unless something were done to stop it. Jules could literally bleed to death in a matter of seconds. Drawing strength from she knew not what reserve, she pulled herself around to face his leg.

There were two principal methods recommended in her first aid classes for stopping bleeding—applying direct pressure on the wound and elevating it to make it harder for the blood to flow out. The pressure method was out; it was impossible for her to lift her arm enough to bring it down on top of his leg. By scraping her arm along the ground, however, she was able to get it under her brother's leg, thus lifting it a little off the ground. Even that little bit was enough to do the trick, though, for the twenty-five gee field was now working in her favor; it pulled the blood downward and reduced the outward flow to a mere trickle.

Because Jules was unconscious and Yvette was otherwise occupied, neither of them saw any more of the action for the next several minutes. If they had, however, they would have been very proud of their relatives. Only that one guard had been able to beat any of the d'Alemberts into action. Rick d'Alembert did not wait to get to his feet to fire his blaster; he shot from a prone position. Soon the air was filled with blaster beams as DesPlainians on both sides managed to squeeze off shots. In the ensuing awkward, slow-motion battle eighteen men died—ten of them being the Grand Duke's last guards. Then, with the opposition gone, the d'Alemberts had only the gravity to contend with. Step by leaden step, Rick pulled his way along the wall into the guard's room. His brain was foggy and his eyes were not focusing properly, but he did manage to find the ultragrav controls. The next instant, he had restored the tunnel to one Earth's gravity—light by his standards, but he was thinking of Jules and two other wounded men.

The instant the ultragrav let up, Yvette gulped in a few deep breaths of air, then ripped the shirt off the dead man on the other side of her brother. She held that compress in place until the flow of blood had abated, then tied it on the burn with a bandage. The wound was a ghastly one, but she was sure that Jules would be able to recover from it.

Rick had fainted after his tremendous exertion in turning off the ultragrav, but fortunately his special strength was no longer needed. The regular army and Service agents could handle the job from this point. In the opposite wall, behind the ruins of the table where the guards had sat, was a large steel vault. The attackers made no attempt to unlock it; such niceties no longer counted at this stage of the game. Demolition experts brought up their shields and sandbags and blew the face of the vault to bits. They removed the debris, ransacked the interior—and found a scroll rolled up on the topmost shelf.

Hearts in their throats and scarcely daring to breathe,

the people who had done so much of the fighting up until now looked on while the handwriting and documentation experts had their turn at center stage. They scrutinized the parchment in minute detail and subjected it to every test they could manage on their portable equipment. "This is the genuine Patent," the chief examiner announced finally; and in the joyous clamor that followed even the dead were for the moment forgotten.

The rest of the operation went so smoothly as to be almost anticlimactic. At a single code word from the major in charge of the Castle Englewood invasion, the full regiment of Imperial Guards sealed the Imperial Palace tighter than Korsho's mailed fist. The Navy assigned two dozen ships to fly in formation over Moscow and create an umbrella impervious to attack. A special team of couriers was dispatched from Castle Englewood to the Imperial Palace, carrying with it the notorious Patent. The instant that was delivered safely into the hands of the Empress Pro Tem, Fleet Admiral Armstrong himself led a company of space marines into the Grand Ballroom and broke up the party by placing Grand Duke Nicholas and his entire retinue under immediate arrest for treason.

The Grand Duke was taken at once to the Pacific Island to confront the Emperor himself. As Stanley Ten watched, his own personal physician administered the nitrobarb to his long-unrecognized half-brother. Then Zander von Wilmenhorst came forward to conduct the intensive questioning that the situation required. Slowly but surely, the full story emerged.

Banion had been placed in an orphanage by his mother when he was slightly over two years old, and had eventually been raised by a foster family that knew nothing of his royal ancestry. Aimée Amorat who kept the Patent hidden herself, and kept equally close tabs on her son as he grew and matured. Finally, when he was sixteen years old, she had come to him and told him the true story of his birth. He hadn't believed her at first, but she had all the proof at hand to convince him—including the Patent, the most conclusive evidence of all. She told him that the Throne and the Empire were his for the taking if he wanted them badly enough; his heritage would depend on his own skill and cunning.

She left the Patent of Royalty with him and then vanished. Though he was to search every corner of the Empire for the next fifty years, there simply was no trace of her to be found. It was as if the Beast of Durward had been swallowed up by the Universe.

But the dream she had left with him had conquered his soul. By the time he was twenty years old, he had already formulated his first tentative plans for galactic domination. By age thirty he had built up a small but intensely loyal organization and was reaping enough profits to allow him to approach Grand Duchess Olga of Sector Twenty. Shrewd woman that she was, she saw the immense benefits to be gained by backing this pretender to the Throne. Their marriage accelerated tremendously the growth of his subversive organization until today, thirty-seven years later, it was undermining and sapping the strength of the entire Empire.

Under the Head's expert probing, Banion revealed all the major hierarchical details of his traitorous organization. With those particulars to work from, the Emperor issued his orders and Fleet Admiral Armstrong carried them out. Since it is much faster in these matters to work from the top down than from the bottom up, full information—including the names of ninety-eight percent of the people involved in the organization—was obtained in less than a week, and the roundup of the miscreants began.

Nicholas and Olga Otamar were tried jointly before the High Court of Justice, with Stanley Ten himself presiding as judge. They were found guilty by a unanimous vote of their peers and were summarily executed. The Dowager Duchess Tanya was also tried and found guilty of abetting treason. She was sentenced to death, but that sentence was commuted to life imprisonment on Gastonia and loss of all titles in exchange for her renewed vow of loyalty to the Crown. Other participants in the conspiracy received sentences ranging from death to several years in prison, depending on the degree of their involvement.

The vacancies in the various services that resulted from this housecleaning operation were many and terribly shocking, but the menace that had hung like a cloud over the Empire for sixty-seven years was at long last ended. And most importantly—at least to Jules and Yvette d'Alembert —the Service of the Empire was finally scoured clean of even the slightest taint of treason.

CHAPTER 14

The Imperial Stars

Because of their high intelligence, their superbly catlike agility, their hair-trigger speed of reaction and their enormous physical strength, DesPlainians were always in demand as fighters, bodyguards and spies. They had been the best secret service agents of, in turn, the Central Intelligence of Earth, the Galactic Intelligence Agency and the Service of the Empire. And of all DesPlainians throughout the years, the d'Alemberts had been by far the best. The fact that the Circus of the Galaxy was SOTE's right arm did not leak from Earth because only the monarch, the Head and a very few of their most highly trusted intimates ever knew it. Nor did it leak from the Circus. Circus people have never spoken to rubes, and the inflexible Code d'Alembert was that d'Alemberts spoke only to d'Alemberts and to the Head. (Unpublished data.)

Again it was late at night. Again the d'Alemberts' Service Special slanted downward through the air toward the roof of the Hall of State of Sector Four. This time, however, the little speedster was not riding a beam and there was no spot of light upon the building's roof. Except for the light of the almost-full moon, everything was dark and still.

Yvette was doing the driving this time. She was now the Yvette of old, shorn of all disguise and artificiality, and wearing what she considered one of her most presentable pants suit ensembles. Jules, again short-haired and smooth-shaven, looked much like his usual self; only the crutch resting beside him gave any indication that he had been affected by this case.

Coming down with scarcely even a bump, Yvette landed

their vehicle near the kiosk of the ultra-private elevator tube. She opened her door and leaped lightly out, then turned to help her brother clamber stiffly and awkwardly out of his side of the car. Duchess Helena came running up to them through the darkness in an extremely unducal fashion.

"Oh, Yvette, I'm so proud of you. You were absolutely *marvelous!*" She put both arms around Yvette's neck and kissed her three times on the lips. "I'm so glad Father let me be the one to come out and meet you. I've been telling him all along that we ought to have more female agents; now maybe he'll listen to me."

Then she turned to Jules, who was standing beside her and smiling in the darkness. Very carefully, so as not to upset his balance, she slipped her arms lightly about his waist and gave him an affectionate hug. "And *you*, Jules! I just can't begin to tell you . . . but *surely* you can hug a girl tighter than *this,* can't you? Even with a bum leg?"

Jules, returning her kisses enthusiastically, tightened his arms a little, but not much. Then, lifting her by the arm-pits, he held her effortlessly out at arms' length with her toes twenty-five centimeters above the ground. "Sure I can," he said with solemn voice but sparkling eyes; "but the trouble is, I never hugged an Earther before and I'm afraid of breaking you in two. It wouldn't be quite *de rigueur,* would it, to break a duchess's back and half her ribs?"

"Oh, there's no danger of *that.* I'm ever so much stronger than . . ." She broke off and her eyes widened in surprise as her hands, already on his arms, tried with all their strength to drive their fingertips into his flesh.

"Oh, I see," she said quietly. "I never quite realized how densely packed you were."

Jules lowered her gently to the roof and she led the way into the elevator tube. She did not tell them why the Head had summoned them here tonight, nor did they ask. She was looking a little thoughtful, and as the three of them started to descend she said timidly, "Jules, I have something to confess. I was all set to fall in love with you and try to arrange to have you fall in love with me. I know I'm reasonably attractive, and . . . well, anyway, when I couldn't even make a dent in those muscles of yours . . . arms as big and hard as those of a heroic-size bronze . . . well . . ." Her voice died away.

Jules smiled at her to ease her embarrassment. "You

couldn't possibly; there's just too much difference. Three gravities is a hell of a lot, and we people of DesPlaines just don't usually marry people who are used to less. I could literally kill you by accident with an overly passionate embrace."

"And besides," Yvette added with light sarcasm, "he's already spoke for. Vonnie'd tear you apart if you made any inroads on her claim."

"But love comes in all sizes, shapes and colors," Jules went on. "We'd be honored to have yours in a less than physical way."

"Oh you do, both of you." Helena's eyes were slightly moist. "Love, friendship, admiration, esteem . . ." She broke off as the elevator door opened.

Stepping aside, she motioned for them to precede her. They took one step each into the Head's private office and stopped dead in their tracks, their eyes and mouths becoming O's of astonishment. For sitting directly before them was the tall, distinguished, gray-haired man who could be none other than Emperor Stanley Ten himself! Beside him, looking equally regal, was the Empress Irene, a statuesque brunette. Over to the side, mixing drinks at the Head's own private bar, was the lithe but prematurely sternfaced Crown Princess Edna. The Head sat casually in a chair across the room, relinquishing control of his desk momentarily to the Emperor.

Stanley Ten stood up and raised a hand in greeting. "No need to kneel," he began—but of course, with their speed of reaction Yvette was already on her knees and Jules, gimpy leg and all, was on one. Their heads were bowed meekly, staring at the carpet.

The Emperor rose from the desk, walked around it and raised the two agents to their feet, kissing Yvette's hand and shaking Jules'. "Formality has its place," he said, "but not privately among friends. During this visit and hereafter in private, I'd like the two of you to call me Bill."

"Oh, we couldn't, Your . . . Sire . . . not possibly," Yvette stammered.

"Not even if I ordered you to?"

"It would take some getting used to," Jules said. "Could we just call you 'sir' for now?"

Stanley Ten smiled—and in that smiling shed a heavy load. "I suppose I understand. Many of the younger generation are not so well bred. 'Sir' will do nicely for now, though I hope in time you will grow to feel more relaxed with me. I take pleasure in presenting you both to my wife, Irene, and to our daughter, Edna."

Introductions made, Edna Stanley went around the room with her tray, serving Jules last. As she handed him his glass of lemonade her dark eyes, usually distant, were soft and warm. "It's a damned, dirty shame," she said with feeling, "that we can't give you two—the two who saved our lives—at least a Grand Imperial Court channeled to every planet in space. And to cap it off, we have to give that stuffed cod Armstrong all the credit. The fathead couldn't smell a conspiracy if it were on his upper lip. But I suppose he'll end up getting the medal you two deserve."

"Well . . ." Jules began, but the Princess rushed on.

"Oh, I know that's the way it has to be, Jules, and I know why. And I know exactly how you feel about it. The Service of the Empire; the fine tradition of the finest group of men and women who ever lived. But knowing all that doesn't make it taste any better or go down any easier. All we can do is thank you for saving all three of our lives—and even that we have to do under cover, or we'll cost you yours."

Overcome with her enthusiasm, she threw her arms around Jules' neck and kissed him warmly. And, while he could not quite bring himself to the point of kissing the Crown Princess of the Empire as though she were an ordinary woman, his response was certainly adequate.

Edna Stanley was not the crying type, but her eyes were brimming as she drew her head back, looked straight into Jules' eyes and went on. "But we three will remember it as long as we live. And the two of you will have a very special place in my heart, always."

Then, without giving Jules a chance to say anything—which was just as well, since he could not possibly have uttered a word—she wriggled free and embraced Yvette. "What do you expect as a reward, dear? Anything within our power is yours. And don't start calling me by any fancy titles; I'm a couple of years younger than you are, and it'd sound silly. Just call me Edna and let it stand at that."

"I'd love to, Edna, it warms me clear through. To be completely honest, all either of us really expected was a pat on the psyche from the Head over there and then another tough job."

From his comfortable chair at one side of the room, the Head gave a low chuckle. "You'll get both, my dear, I can assure you. I have no intention of letting any more cases go as long as this one did before putting the two of you to use. The whole matter might have been handled much more simply—and with fewer repercussions—if I'd called you in several years ago." Then, turning to the Emperor, "You see what I mean, Bill?"

"Very much so. They're d'Alemberts. Metal of proof, wrought and tempered." He turned to Jules and Yvette, and added, "You young people don't realize that your lives are more important to the Empire than mine is."

"I not only don't realize it, sir," Jules said doggedly, "but I don't see how it can possibly be true. You are the third and greatest of the Great Stanleys; Eve and I are only two d'Alemberts out of over a thousand."

"Correction, please. As of now you are—and probably will be for the next decade or so until your replacements mature—the two most capable human beings alive." The Emperor replenished his drink and brought Yvette a small pitcher of fresh orange juice, while Edna waited on the others. "And anything the two of you can't do personally, you have the multiple talents of your family to draw on. But let's examine this 'Great Stanley' business a little, since you brought it up; it'll be a good way to get better acquainted. I've studied my family's history quite thoroughly —enough to have developed what is, to me at least, a new theory. Has it ever occurred to you to wonder why the three so-called Great Stanleys happened to be the three who reigned the longest? Empress Stanley Three, thirty-seven years; Emperor Stanley Six, thirty-six years; and I, who have more than either, and will probably—thanks to your efforts, I'm happy to point out—reign three more before reaching the age of seventy and abdicating in favor of Edna. Have you wondered why that should be?"

"N-o-o-o, sir. I can't say that I have."

"It's a highly pertinent fact. You know, I'm sure, that only one of my predecessors ever managed to die a 'natural' death."

"Yes, sir," Yvette spoke up. "Empress Stanley Three."

Stanley Ten nodded. "And even that was not until after she'd abdicated in favor of her son. My father died in a space accident that all the experts assure me was just that —an accident. The other seven were all assassinated—

usually by their own sons or daughters or brothers or sisters."

"Yes, sir," Jules said. "We know that, too."

"Their problem was a relative one, literally. As for myself, I had only one relative in my own generation: my half-brother, Banion, whom you eliminated as a threat in so noble a fashion. The rest of my predecessors' problem was that they had too many children, too young. To alleviate that, Irene and I decided to have only one child; and even then we waited to have Edna until I was almost forty-five. My advisors had fits about that, claiming that I was jeopardizing the Succession; I suppose if I had died prematurely they might have been right, but as it is I think I've actually strengthened it. As soon as Edna's able to carry the load herself, we'll hand it over to her on a silver platter and step out, so that she won't need to kill us."

"Dad!" the Crown Princess exclaimed. "You know very well I'd never even *think* of such a thing."

"William!" the Empress protested. "What a *nasty* thing to say!"

"I'm sure you haven't thought of it," the Emperor said gently to his daughter. "But that's only because you haven't had to; I always made it clear to you from the first that you would have the title when you were ready for it. If I'd hoarded it to myself, you might have turned out a little greedier. Like begets like. Also the fact that you had no scheming siblings to guard yourself against helped you develop decently, just like it helped me.

"At any rate, Irene, you helped me plan it, and on the whole I'd say it worked out beautifully. I'm sure everyone here has heard the old wheeze that 'power corrupts; absolute power corrupts absolutely'?"

They all had.

"My theory is that only the first part is really true. For, as a matter of fact, no human being ever had absolute power until King Stanley the Sixth crowned himself Emperor Stanley One and took it. He had the whole Galaxy. Every other despot in history was always reaching for more; so the truth of that old saying was never put to the test.

"Indeed, there is much in pre-Empire history that argues against its truth. The worst gangsters and the most rapacious capitalists Earth ever knew, when they got old enough and powerful enough and rich enough, frequently turned from greed and exploitation to something that was for the

141

good of all mankind. And the entire history of the House of Stanley bears this out."

A short silence fell upon the room: then the Empress said thoughtfully, "Well, it's something to think about, at least . . . and it *does* seem to make sense . . . but, my dear, what has all that got to do with the present case?"

"Everything," said Stanley Ten, deadly serious now. "It shows why these two d'Alemberts in particular—highly trained, uniquely gifted, innately and completely loyal to the Empire—are much more important to the realm than I am. Not that they are indispensable; no one is. But they are at present irreplaceable and I am not. Any Stanley who is able to live long enough becomes a Great Stanley by sheer force of circumstance—and Edna will be one from the day she's crowned."

The Emperor turned to face Jules and Yvette. "Nevertheless, my young friends, my life is extremely important to me. It is also important to Irene and Edna, as are their lives to me. The three of us are important to a few really close friends, such as Zander there and your father, the Duke; but you'd be surprised and dismayed to learn just how scarce friends are. The life of any individual Emperor or Empress, however, is of very little importance to the Empire itself, of which its rulers are merely the symbols. It's one of the most comical paradoxes of power that the more you have, the more constrained you are and the less you can do. Sometimes, in my more whimsical moments, I think that the Empire could go on quite nicely without any ruler at all; but then my vanity intervenes and tells me how indispensable I am.

"I do know, however, that the Empire endures only because people such as yourselves are loyal to it. Without that loyalty, the Empire is just an abstract concept that would crumble and fall in an instant. Instead of prosperity and peace there would be widespread and terribly destructive wars of planetary conquest. Without a strong symbol of unity, our present civilization would degenerate into barbarism and savagery.

"We Stanleys do what we can, but in the final analysis the Empire rests squarely upon the arch of the various services—and your Service of the Empire is the very keystone of that arch.

"As Edna said, it's a great shame that we three can give you only our thanks. It isn't, however, just the thanks of

142

three people, but rather that of an entire Empire." He took the d'Alemberts' right hands, one in each of his own, and shook them vigorously. Jules and Yvette were speechless, each with tears in his eyes.

"I'd like to propose a salute to the two best of us in the entire room," the Emperor concluded. He raised his glass in the direction of the two magnificent agents. "Here's to tomorrow, fellows and friends. May we all live to see it!"